The Danger
Next Door

Kris Langman

Post Hoc Publishing

Chapter One

B ANG. BANG. BANG.

Anne groaned and squashed her pillow up against her ears.

Bang. Bang. Bang.

Rolling over, she squinted at the glowing red numbers on her alarm clock: 4:05 a.m. She slid reluctantly out of bed, yanking down her 'Programmers Do It In Code' T-shirt. As she stumbled out into the living room she heard yelling coming from the other side of her front door.

"Let me in, you bastard!" It was a man's voice, completely sloshed.

Bang. Bang. Bang.

Anne paused, listening. He wasn't pounding on her door. The commotion seemed to be directed at the apartment next to hers.

Bang. Bang . . . her neighbor's door creaked open.

"Yes?" The voice was unemotional, precise. Drunken visitors at 4:00 a.m. did not disturb it in the least.

"Finally. Christ, Davidson. Do you sleep with your head up your ass?"

"As a rule, no." The voice hovered between mild amusement and contempt. "What do you want, Jimmy?"

"Let me in, give me a drink, and I'll tell you. Or I could just stand here in the hall and announce to all your lovely neighbors that I'm cutting off your money supply."

A long pause. Anne held her breath, afraid they could hear her through the door.

"Come in," she heard her neighbor say calmly, and then the door shut.

THREE HOURS LATER Anne groaned again. The alarm clock was beeping insistently. She sighed and pulled the duvet over her head, then quickly threw it off again. It smelled like last week's pizza. With anchovies. Laundry day was definitely overdue. She stretched down to the end of the bed for her pink terrycloth bathrobe, giving it a sniff as she pulled it on. Not too bad. A hint of last night's chicken tikka masala, but she could live with it for another week.

She yawned and trudged into the kitchen to forage for breakfast. The cupboards were discouragingly empty. She'd have to stop at Sainsburys after work. She tried the fridge. Cold pizza. And one last Diet Coke. The breakfast of champions. She tucked the Diet Coke can into a pocket of her robe and took a quick peek out the sliding glass door which led to her terrace. Concrete tubs of geraniums shared the small balcony with rusting patio furniture. The tubs overflowed with rainwater, delighting the local sparrows. They splashed and fluttered in the muddy water like college freshman in a hot tub on Spring Break. It was Jacuzzis, skinny-dipping, and sleazy sparrow pickup lines.

Anne took her pizza and coke into the bedroom and flopped onto the bed for some channel surfing. Her tiny TV was perched precariously atop a steamer trunk at the end of the bed. She had rented the flat furnished, and the trunk was symptomatic of the landlord's decorating style – trying too hard to impress. The trunk was huge, with copper rivets and an embossed leather top. It looked like something a Vanderbilt would have taken on the Titanic. The Chagall print on the wall opposite the bed was there to show that the flat's owner had a cultural side, but it was obvious that the large blue goat leering from the center of the painting preferred the crude to the cultured.

After five minutes of the news on BBC1 – another Tube strike – Anne switched over to GMTV. One of the Spice Girls – who knew which one (the ability to name all of the group's members was strictly a British talent) – was discussing her love life in earnest tones. Anne gulped the last of the Diet Coke and pushed herself reluctantly off the bed.

Ten minutes later her get-ready-for-work routine was finished. Brush teeth. Wash face. Pee. Put on underwear, jeans, T-shirt, and Nikes. Check all of the above for holes, mud, and ink spots. Ignore any holes, mud, or ink spots found.

Anne ran a comb through her straight dark hair, wincing as two long silvery strands glinted in the harsh bathroom light. She grabbed a pair of tweezers and yanked the offenders out. Thirty-three was way too young to be going gray. It was early February, and the gray days of her first winter in London had her pale skin looking even whiter than usual. She slapped herself on each cheek to get the blood flowing. Her large green eyes had dark circles under them, the result of last night's disturbed slumber. A stop at Starbucks for an extra-large vanilla latte was in order.

She wandered into the living room in search of her parka. It wasn't in its usual heap on the sofa. Nope, not under the kitchen table. It couldn't possibly be . . . she went back into the bedroom and opened the closet. Amazing. She shrugged the jacket on and grabbed her purse off the night table next to her bed. She swung it over her shoulder and then paused, pressing her ear against the front door.

She strained her ears for any hint of noise in the hallway, in particular the ponderous tread of Mrs. Emily Watson. Mrs. Watson was seventy-two and lived two doors down. Anne had to pass her door if she wanted to take the lift, which was why she generally took the stairs. Mrs. Watson had an uncanny ability to pick up the sound of any hapless soul passing by her door, no matter how stealthy their tread. Her bait was freshly baked cinnamon scones. The prey would innocently reach for a scone and a cuppa, and the trap was sprung. Hours would pass before they escaped, writhing in torment at the graphic details of Georgie's last poo. Georgie being Mrs. Watson's three-year-old grandson, recently potty trained.

Anne eased open the door and poked her head out. A quick look left and right. All clear. She set off along the carpeted hallway at a brisk pace, heading for the stairs, but was brought to a limping halt by her left knee, which had locked up. It was an old injury from her college days on the UCLA cross-country team. The extra mile she had jogged on her lunch hour yesterday must have aggravated it. Anne shook her leg to loosen the joint, but it was no use. The pain was persistent. She sighed and reversed course, heading for the lift. The lifts at the Barbican were small and cramped. Mrs. Watson avoidance wasn't the only reason she didn't use them. Her building, Andrewes House, was not one of the Barbican's giant tower blocks, but its population was big enough to cause occasional rush-hour squish in the lifts.

Today she was in luck. Only one person waited in the lobby. Her next door neighbor, Dr. Danielson, Dr. Davidson, Dr. Something. The sight of him reminded Anne of last night's disturbance. He nodded to her briefly as she approached and then turned away. He wasn't the friendliest of neighbors, but then neither was she. Anne preferred his reserve to the hook 'em and reel 'em in approach of Mrs. Watson.

She studied him surreptitiously, wondering who last night's drunken visitor had been. Possibly a patient. Dr. Daniel . . . no, she was pretty sure it was Davidson. Dr. Davidson. He was a psychiatrist, or a psychologist. She could never remember what the difference was. She had only met him once before, three months ago, when she had just moved in. They had arrived at the floor's trash chute at the same time and he had offered a perfunctory handshake. He had manicured nails and unusually soft hands for a man. His transparent blue eyes and white-blond hair gave him a Swedish appearance. His clothes were always tailored and expensive looking. Today he had on an immaculate gray suit, powder blue shirt, and pale blue silk tie. His sartorial perfection made Anne uncomfortably aware of the large blackberry jam stain on the sleeve of her jacket. As an elbow rest, toast with jam was comfortable but decidedly messy.

The ping of an electronic bell bounced off the marble floor of the lobby. The lift had arrived. Anne followed Dr. Davidson in and stood stiffly in front of him, facing the doors. A scratched safety placard pasted on the door informed her that taking the stairs when the building was on fire would be to her benefit. This point was driven home by a stick figure standing in a box (the doomed lift, presumably). Flames shot out of the figure's head. Apparently the Barbican's lifts were prone to re-enacting biblical scenes of the damned.

Anne disliked lifts, even when they weren't on fire. It was weird being in such a confined space with strangers. No way out until the doors opened. Anything could happen. Things like . . . out of the corner of her eye Anne saw a gray pin-striped arm reach out and push the emergency stop button. Things like that, for instance.

The lift shuddered to a halt, creaking in protest at the interruption. Anne turned around, taking an involuntary step backward. Dr. Davidson was watching her, one pale hand adjusting the Rolex Oyster on his left wrist. His fingers were completely hairless, as if he'd waxed them.

"I hope we didn't disturb you last night," he said.

"Pardon?"

"My inebriated guest last night. All the yelling. He must have woken you up."

"No, not at all. I mean, if he did I don't remember." She nodded in what she hoped was a casual manner at the lift buttons. "I think we should get going again, don't you?" When he didn't respond Anne reached a hand out toward the buttons.

"Not yet."

Anne froze. She forced herself to look him in the eye. She had to look up. He was five foot ten or eleven to her five foot five. At least he was under six feet. For some reason this felt important, as if one or two inches meant the difference between safety and danger.

He took a step toward her and leaned in. Anne fought the impulse to move away and stood her ground. She was darn proud of herself. Dr. Davidson smiled slightly at her efforts.

"I just want to make it clear that I value my privacy," he said quietly. His aftershave smelled like ice. "It would upset me if I found out that people in this building were gossiping about my personal affairs."

Anne bristled. As if. She had better things to do with her time than to stand around gossiping about her neighbors. She glared at him.

"I have no intention of doing any such thing," she said. "Your affairs are not that interesting."

Dr. Davidson smiled briefly. "Good," he said. He stepped away from her and pressed the button for the ground floor. The lift jolted into motion. When they reached the bottom and the doors opened Anne jumped out like a racehorse from the starting gate. She darted away, not looking back. Pushing through the lobby doors she emerged into the cold, rainy London morning and let out her breath in a whoosh. Her shoulders were up to her ears with tension. She did a little dance on the sidewalk, jogging in place and shaking her shoulders. It had always helped to calm her nerves before a big race, and it helped now. She set off for work with only a tiny trickle of anxiety slithering down her back.

IT WAS ONLY a ten-minute walk from Anne's flat in the Barbican to her office in Finsbury Circus, but the rain was heavy enough to soak through her parka. The unpleasant encounter in the lift had been on continuous replay in her head, her collapsible umbrella forgotten at the bottom of her purse. By the time she dashed past the Moorgate tube station and into the lane leading to Finsbury Circus she was soaked through.

Dodging a kamikaze bike messenger barreling along the sidewalk, Anne dashed up a broad flight of stone steps and into the marble lobby of Britannic House. Dominating the north side of Finsbury Circus, Britannic House was a listed building – which meant that a committee of nameless bureaucrats had deemed it chock full of historical and architectural worthiness. Its white stone façade had recently been steam-cleaned, and the whole building shone like a backlit milk bottle. Anne swerved around the potted palms in the lobby and ran up the wide central staircase in an effort to warm herself up, gritting her teeth at the sharp pain in her knee. One of these days she was going to get it fixed. Of course, that day would only come when her fear of doctors was less than the pain in her knee.

She slowed to a walk on the third-floor landing and shook out her knee. The company she worked for, The Franklin Group, had a small suite of offices at the end of the landing. They did contract software design for banks and insurance companies in the financial district of London, known as the City. The company employed eight program-mers and several support staff. Anne was one of their senior programmers, with ten years of experience.

It was only 8:00 a.m. when she entered the company's reception area, but receptionist Lindsey Maxwell was already at her post. If Meet and Greet were an Olympic sport, Lindsey would own the gold. She was always immaculately dressed and made up, every long tawny hair in place. In Lindsey's presence Anne invariably felt like a hedgehog with a bad haircut (the SuperCuts version). To be fair,

Lindsey was always perfectly polite to her, though Anne had noticed a few pitying glances thrown her way. Usually on days when she was wearing something inside out. Lindsey was wise to the 'it's a fashion statement' excuse.

"Good morning, Anne. A bit wet out isn't it?"

"Just a bit," acknowledged Anne, wringing a small waterfall out of the sleeve of her jacket.

"I keep a blow dryer here for emergencies," said Lindsey, pulling a large and scary looking appliance out of her desk drawer. "It's 2000 watts. It'll dry out your clothes in minutes." She handed it to Anne.

"Thanks, Lindsey. I'll bring it right back."

"Oh, no hurry."

Now heavily armed, Anne made herself a cup of tea with sugar to replace the forgotten Starbucks latte and took it into her small office. The tiny room had a mildew smell coming from the carpet and an ill-conceived skylight which leaked when it rained, but every time she entered she was reminded of her good fortune. Most offices in the City were ghastly open-plan affairs, noisy and crowded, with dozens of desks crammed together in rows. No privacy, and no escape from your neighbor's intimate phone conversations with their girl-friend/boyfriend/psychic/urologist. Her own office was an oasis of peace by comparison. Its best feature was the large window which looked down onto the square below. Two desks faced each other next to the window.

Anne had to share the room with only one other person, Nick Cooper, programmer extraordinaire. At least he liked to think so. He wasn't as good as he thought he was, but he wasn't bad. Just a little too cocky, as only a twenty-three-year-old boy could be. They got along okay now, though at first Anne had mistaken him for another employee's teenage son. With his skinny frame and floppy blond hair he looked six years younger than he was. He was also prone to a bastardized version of Valley Speak ('dude' was his favorite word), which Anne found more than a little ironic. She had been born and raised in the Valley itself (San Fernando, the one and only), while she knew for a fact that Nick was a product of Basingstoke, a very un-California-like city in the southeast of England.

She set the tea down on her desk and turned on the blow dryer. When she aimed the blast of hot air at her face its force nearly gave her whiplash. Drying out took only ten minutes from top to toe. Even her jeans were warm and toasty. She returned the dryer to Lindsey and returned to her desk for her morning ritual of tea drinking and staring out the window. She had a bird's eye view of the bowling green in the center of Finsbury Circus, a circle-shaped park surrounded by both modern and nineteenth-century office buildings. No one ever seemed to use the bowling green, despite the existence of a small building in front of the green called the Finsbury Circus Bowling Club, with rows of metal Bocci-type balls lined up in readiness. The park around the green was bare now, its large maples leafless, its flowerbeds muddy plots of turned-over earth, but in the spring the London Parks department bedded out masses of orange tulips and pink cyclamen. Anne had admired them last year on her first business trip to London. She'd been working in the Franklin Group's Los Angeles headquarters, and when a chance to transfer to the London office had come up she'd jumped at it. The company was paying half of the rent for her flat in the Barbican, an arrangement for which she was extremely grateful. A bit of flat-hunting when she'd first arrived in London had nearly caused her to pass out from sticker shock. An entire house – with pool – in LA could be had for the same price as a one-room London studio.

"Hey, dudette." Nick rushed in and threw his backpack on his desk then flopped into his long-suffering chair. It groaned in protest.

Anne turned away from the window. "Good Morning."

"Oh man, what a weekend. The curls at Newquay were like three feet high. Rad." He stretched both scrawny arms over his head to illustrate the giant waves which had crashed over him.

Anne smiled indulgently. She was no surfer, but she was pretty sure that three feet didn't constitute major wave action. Well, anywhere in the world other than Cornwall. And when had 'rad' come back into fashion?

"Should I release version two of that app for Barclays today?" asked Nick, running a hand through his blond hair in a vain attempt to get it out of his eyes. He had recently started putting some kind of gel in it, and pieces stuck up like new-mown hay.

"Not yet," replied Anne. "Two of the asset allocation functions have bugs in them. I should have them fixed by the end of today."

"Okay. I'll create some test data, and maybe work on the install program. Hey, check out my new duds."

Nick launched himself off his chair and bounded over to Anne's desk. He pulled at the sides of a pair of extremely baggy surfers shorts, which boasted a pattern of fat red pineapples. The shorts fell to an unfortunate length just past Nick's non-existent calf-muscles, exposing two shins so white and scrawny they looked like peeled leeks.

"Got 'em at a flea market in Camden. Only two quid. Hard to believe, huh?"

Anne could only nod in open-mouth acquiescence.

THE REST OF the workday was filled with the usual code testing and debugging. Entertainment was provided by Nick, who decided to show Anne and Lindsey the finer points of a cut-back, using one of the reception area's chairs as a surfboard. The demo was going well, until Nick overestimated his board's stability and crashed head first onto reception's glass-topped coffee table. The table was uninjured, but a potted cactus atop a stack of ComputerWorlds had a narrow escape. An inch to the left and it would have been an unwilling participant in intimate relations with Nick's nose.

Anne left the office as usual at 5:30 that evening. The smell of wet stone and soggy leaves rose up from the pavement. She walked briskly down London Wall, dodging her fellow pedestrians at every step, her umbrella tilting from side to side as it jostled for space. Even after three months she still wasn't used to how crowded the London sidewalks were. She never managed to walk in a straight line for more than ten steps.

After a long wait at the light on Moorgate Street she dashed under the painted wooden grapes hanging over the Kings Head pub and ran up a narrow metal stairway which lead to the St. Alphage highwalk. These highwalks criss-crossed the City like giant spiderwebs. St. Alphage's walk connected to the Barbican complex, leading to a confusing series of pedestrian bridges and walkways winding through the gray concrete buildings. First-time visitors invariably got lost. Anne still took the occasional wrong turn. At the top of the stairs she turned onto the highwalk, passing The Plough, an ugly modern pub which Anne had christened the Anti-Pub. No leaded windows or cozy Victorian woodwork for The Plough. It seemed to delight in its concrete and metal ugliness. Anne had never gone in, afraid that the inside would be even worse than the outside.

After a few more twists and turns she reached her apartment building, Andrewes House. It was blocky, concrete, and unremarkable except for the balconies belonging to each flat, which all overlooked the artificial lake in the center of the Barbican complex. As Anne opened the blue metal door of the Andrewes House stairwell a distinctly alcoholic aroma met her nose. She looked around, wondering if one of the area's homeless had wandered in. The smell increased as she entered the hallway leading to her flat. A man was knocking on her neighbor's door, and as she approached the source of the smell became apparent. The man reeked of gin, bourbon, whiskey, something in the alcohol family. Anne didn't drink, and so couldn't identify the culprit, but the man appeared to have bathed in it. With his clothes on.

"Hey, do you know this son of a bitch?"

Anne paused briefly, and then continued past him to her own front door. "Pardon?" she asked cautiously. She recognized his voice. He was the drunk from last night. The voice was the same, but his appearance didn't match the image of him which had formed in her mind. His accent sounded vaguely lower class and East End Cockney, but Anne wondered if this was just an affectation. Some upper-class British men were into the Mockney thing, affecting a Cockney accent to seem tougher than they really were, and apart from his voice everything about this guy screamed public school. His tan overcoat and chocolate blazer both looked like cashmere, probably hand-stitched in some little shop off Jermyn Street, and, while Anne was no expert when it came to labels, she was pretty sure his loafers were Gucci. His clothes fit beautifully but didn't suit him. The overall effect was that of a boy who had raided his father's closet. Barely taller than she was, he had a pale complexion and a delicate frame which didn't match his belligerent voice.

"I need to talk to the doc. Do you know when he'll be home?"

"Sorry," said Anne. "I don't." She fished her keys out of her purse.

"But you know him pretty well, being next-door neighbors and everything," the man persisted.

"I don't know him at all. We've only spoken twice," Anne replied, turning away to unlock her door.

"Hello, Jimmy," said a voice behind her, startling Anne so much that she dropped her keys. Her hand shook as she picked them up.

"Hey, doc. Got any more of that single malt? I need a top up." Jimmy was swaying so much he looked ready to break into the Twist.

Dr. Davidson glanced at Jimmy briefly and then focused on Anne. "Hello, Miss Lambert."

Anne started. She wasn't aware that he knew her surname.

"I see you've met Jimmy. The Honorable James Soames, I should say. Not much of a prize is he, despite the title."

Anne eyed him warily, the encounter in the lift still vivid. She expected him to make his excuses and disappear into his flat, with or without Jimmy, so the next thing he said came as a shock.

"Why don't you come in for a drink? You and Jimmy both. We'll all get acquainted."

She was so surprised by this unexpected invitation that Anne found herself being shepherded through his front door before she could think up a reason to decline. Jimmy followed her in, clutching at the door frame for support. Dr. Davidson turned the deadbolt after he closed the door. Anne looked around warily. The theme of the decor was understated luxury. Her feet sunk into a plush gray carpet. Frosted glass sconces in Art Deco shapes provided just the right amount of illumination. The coffee table in the middle of the room, a solid block of Lucite, resembled a giant ice cube. The sofa and chairs grouped around it were sculpted out of chrome tubing and gray leather. The room was cold, as if the heat hadn't been on for weeks.

"Please sit down." Dr. Davidson pointed at the sofa in a way that suggested arresting officer rather than host. Anne reluctantly crossed to it and perched on its edge. Jimmy fell into the armchair across from her.

"Can I offer you something to drink?"

"Whiskey," came Jimmy's immediate reply.

Anne shook her head. The doctor poured Jimmy's drink and one for himself. He carried them over and set them down on the Lucite table with a sharp clink. Jimmy grabbed his and gulped it down.

"So, what were you two talking about?" asked Dr. Davidson as he took a seat on the sofa next to Anne. She leaned away from him, the fingers of her left hand curling inward.

"Pardon?" she asked.

"In the hallway just now. The two of you were chatting away like old friends."

Jimmy gave a short, bitter laugh. The look in his hazel eyes was surprisingly perceptive for someone so drunk. "The doc doesn't like people talking about him. He's afraid things will come out. Nasty things."

Dr. Davidson stared at him impassively, as if daring him to continue. Jimmy looked like he was considering it, but then decided on the safer option of fetching himself another drink. He lurched over to the bar and returned with a bottle of Drambuie.

"We weren't chatting away. We barely exchanged two sentences," said Anne, annoyance overcoming her nervousness. How many times was she going to have to justify herself to this guy? He should look up the word 'paranoia'.

"So, you're some kind of doctor?" she asked, just to break the silence which stretched like skin pulled too tight.

"I'm a psychologist. I have a practice in the City, just off Old Broad Street."

"What, you treat suicidal stock brokers when the FTSE 100 drops a few too many percentage points?" Anne tried to paste an interested expression on her face, but could feel Sullen and Defensive battling for control of her features.

"Sometimes." The doctor carefully unclasped his Rolex and laid it on the transparent surface of the coffee table, where it glittered like a silver minnow in a frozen pond. "Mainly I treat people with addiction problems, like Jimmy here. Addiction is the thing to specialize in. You never run out of clients."

"That's kind of a money-grubbing attitude, isn't it?" asked Anne.

Jimmy laughed, choking on his drink and spitting droplets of whiskey onto the plush gray carpet. "She's got you pegged, doc." He winked conspiratorially at Anne. "There's nothing the doc likes better than lots of lovely, lovely cash. He'd bathe in it if he could."

Dr. Davidson stared at him until Jimmy again backed down. He teased a snowy handkerchief out of his breast pocket and made a show of mopping amber drops of whiskey off the coffee table.

Another long silence filled the room. Her host showed no interest in breaking it, so Anne decided it was a good time to make her escape.

She stood up. "I have to be going," she said, politely but firmly. She headed for the door, Jimmy watching and Dr. Davidson following. The doctor didn't say anything until her hand was on the doorknob.

"Wait," he said, leaning casually against the door, arms folded. "I apologize if I've offended you. I overreact sometimes. It's just that in my line of work I need to protect my reputation. Gossip could cost me patients, or even my license. I'm sure you understand."

"Not really," said Anne, stubbornly refusing to look at him. She stood holding the doorknob, staring down at her hand. They remained like that for what seemed to Anne a ridiculously long time. Finally, Dr. Davidson reached in front of her and opened the deadbolt.

Chapter Two

A NNE WAS FEELING chipper. She'd managed to avoid Dr. Davidson for over a week. On top of that it was Saturday and the sun was shining. She wrapped her bathrobe around her and took a poppy seed bagel out onto her terrace. She munched it while admiring the artificial lake in the courtyard below. Its algae-green water glowed with a weird phosphorescence where the sunlight touched it. On cloudy days the Barbican's gray concrete buildings were unremittingly dreary, but on the rare days when the sun shone the complex looked, well, not exactly cheerful, but at least fresh and avant-garde. It had won a few architecture awards upon its completion in the 1980's. In addition to its large blocks of flats a theatre complex sprawled across the north side of its central courtyard. Anne had been to see The Merchant of Venice in a small theatre in its basement called The Pit. She'd also attended a rather flashy version of Hamlet in the large main auditorium. She couldn't honestly call herself a Shakespeare fan, but she felt obligated to get a bit of culture while in London. Obligated to who she wasn't quite sure.

Such a warm, sunny day in February was not to be wasted. A walk along the Thames was in order. She went back inside and stood surveying the living room. The beige carpet was speckled with dark spots of dirt like the chips in a chocolate chip cookie, and the coffee table was sprinkled with dust, but otherwise the flat looked respectable enough (if you didn't go into the kitchen). Housekeeping chores could wait until next weekend. Of course, next weekend she would probably come to the same conclusion.

A cheap reproduction of Van Gogh's Sunflowers hung crookedly over the patched suede sofa. Anne straightened it. The housekeeping gods were now appeased.

She threw on jeans, a black t-shirt, Nikes, and her favorite North Face parka. A deep forest green and waterproof, it had a large hood which came in handy when out in the English weather. She stuffed her keys and wallet in the pocket of her jeans and opened the front door.

Idiot! Anne mentally smacked herself upside the head. She hadn't been on Mrs. Watson alert, and sure enough, there she was – all paisley silk and bouffant blue hair. She had snagged poor harmless Mr. Carter from down the hall. He was edging away from her, but she kept edging right along with him. They looked like ill-matched dance partners having their first foxtrot lesson. His desperate sideways glances changed to joy when he spotted Anne. She knew exactly what he was thinking – shift the predator's attention to other prey. Well, not this time buddy. She put her head down and high-tailed it toward the stairs.

"Oh, Anne . . . Anne dear."

Damn! Just keep moving. Just a few more feet to freedom.

"Anne dear, come here please. I must show you my new snaps of Georgie. They've turned out beautifully."

Anne stopped, shoulders sagging. She knew she was beaten. She turned and headed for the lion's mouth. Maybe it would be quick and painless this time.

FORTY-FIVE MINUTES LATER Anne was on her sixth ginger biscuit, third cup of over-sugared Earl Grey, and twenty-seventh snapshot of Georgie grinning maniacally from the depths of a yellow plastic wading pool.

"Here's one of my little sweetheart looking so clever. You can just tell he's going to grow up to be an intellectual. A poet perhaps, or a painter. A real painter, of course. Darling little landscapes, with thatched cottages. None of this modern nonsense which looks the same no matter whether you hang it upside down or right side up. More tea, dear?"

"No thank you, Mrs. Watson. I really must be go . . ."

"Oh my goodness. I nearly forgot. Georgie did the most adorable finger painting. Mr. Amin from number 212 said it reminded him of an early Picasso. You simply must see it. It's on the refrigerator. I'll just fetch it and put the kettle on again."

She disappeared into the kitchen, leaving Anne to wonder which Mr. Amin was more adept at – lying or art criticism. She glanced speculatively at the front door. Did she dare? Yes. No. Maybe. Gaagh! At times good manners were a definite handicap. She sighed and slumped back into her chair, gazing listlessly at the chintz and figurines covering every available surface in Mrs. Watson's overheated 'parlour'. Possibly the mating of a Laura Ashley factory outlet and the gift shop at Buckingham Palace had produced other offspring, but this room was its prodigal.

A copy of the Daily Mail lay on the end table next to her over-stuffed armchair. Anne picked it up and glanced at the headlines. The usual debates over government spending.

A picture at the bottom of the page caught her eye. A head shot of a man in his twenties or thirties, possibly a formal portrait. He looked familiar. She skimmed the short paragraph below the picture. 'Drowning victim pulled out of the Thames, near Greenwich. The Honorable James Soames, beloved son of Sir Jack Soames and Lady Belinda Soames.' Jimmy! Anne shivered. She had talked to the guy only a week ago, and now he was dead. She hadn't liked him much, but still. An acquaintance of Jimmy's – a man by the name of Rick 'Razor' Billingsley – was 'helping the police with their inquiries'.

Anne absentmindedly re-folded the paper and put it back on the end table. 'Helping the police with their inquiries.' She had read enough Agatha Christie to know that this meant the police considered 'Razor' a suspect in Jimmy's death. She wondered why. Jimmy had obviously chosen drink as his calling. He could easily have fallen into the river while drunk. Leaned too far over a railing, stumbled off the end of a dock.

"Here we are. This is one of Georgie's best. It just screams talent, don't you think?" Mrs. Watson approached, holding a large sheet of paper aloft like a ceremonial banner. She laid the heirloom reverently in Anne's lap and then stepped back, her liver-spotted hands clasped at her chin.

Anne looked down at the pink and red splodges squirming across the paper. It looked like open-heart surgery courtesy of Bride of Chucky.

"It's lovely Mrs. Watson. Really. Now, I'm afraid I must be going. I have some errands to run." Anne stood and began the perilous journey to the front door. Mrs. Watson was infamous for throwing herself into the path of departing guests like an over-zealous Secret Service agent. Today, however, Anne got off easy. She was out the door after only ten more minutes of urgent Georgie updates. Anne breathed a deep sigh of relief as she crossed the threshold and headed off for her walk, only an hour later than planned.

ANNE STROLLED DOWN London Wall and turned right onto Old Broad Street, dodging around a muddy pit smack in the middle of the sidewalk, just one small piece of London's unending jigsaw puzzle of scaffolding, construction sites, and pedestrian-hostile obstacles. She followed Old Broad Street it until it merged with Threadneedle, passing the imposing columns of the Royal Exchange and the massive bulk of the Bank of England. The streets of the City were blessedly deserted. Everything in London's Square Mile shut down on the weekends – shops, offices, tube stations. It was a pleasure to walk unimpeded down the empty sidewalks. She passed the One Poultry building, which sat at the corner of Poultry Street and Cheapside. The building grinned cheekily at the Bank of England across the way. One Poultry was a fantastical, Dr. Seuss-like confection of red and tan stripes flowing around odd angles. The building seemed to thumb its nose at the cluster of dignified stone buildings in front of it. The Bank of England, Mansion House, and the Royal Exchange in their turn undoubtedly felt that One Poultry was not quite 'their sort'.

As she approached the ornate steel arches of Blackfriars bridge Anne passed the figure of a dragon, about two feet high, painted gray and perched atop a pedestal, its wings spread wide, its snarling mouth painted red. One of the guardians of the City. At each entrance into the Square Mile these fierce little sentinels kept watch. In times past if the King or Queen wanted to enter the City they had to obtain permission from the Lord Mayor to cross its borders. A quote popped into Anne's mind as she passed the statue: 'Beyond this point there be dragons.' The ancient saying referred to unknown terrors lurking at the edge of the seas, but the modern world had its own share of dragons. Dr. Davidson could surely spout a flame or two. Even Mrs. Watson could emit a few puffs of smoke.

AN HOUR LATER Anne hummed her favorite bit from Tchaikovsky's Slavonic March as she opened her mailbox and pulled out two envelopes. The walk along the river in the sun had cheered her up. After living in the LA sunshine all her life the perpetually gray skies of London tended to leave her feeling a bit draggy. She glanced at the mail while climbing the stairs. One envelope was her British Telecom phone bill. The other was a mystery. She frowned at it and turned it over. Nothing. It was completely blank, both back and front. She unlocked the door to her flat and leaned against it while opening the blank envelope. On a single sheet of plain white typing paper a few handwritten lines zigzagged wildly across the page.

'I JUST WANTED you to know who you're living next door to. He's hurt a lot of people. He got to me years ago. At school. Wyndham Prep. Ask him about Wyndham Prep.'

NO SIGNATURE. ANNE turned the sheet over. An address was scrawled there: Flat B, 116 Wardour, Soho. She flipped it back over and read it through again, then stood staring blankly down at it. What was it exactly? A warning? A threat? A cry for help? A practical joke? She had no idea who'd written it, but it seemed to refer to Dr. Davidson. Unless someone had it in for Mr. Golan, the tenant on the other side of her. As Mr. Golan was ninety-three, blind, and bedridden, this seemed unlikely.

She glanced down at the note again, and then at the wall separating her flat from Dr. Davidson's. The conversation she had overheard more than a week ago came back to her. Jimmy shouting something about money. 'I'm going to cut off your money supply.' Money supply suggested regular payments. Possibly blackmail. That damn doctor. Every time she thought of him her shoulders started climbing up to her ears. She tucked the sheet of paper back into its envelope and stuck it into a fat book of data processing algorithms that lay open on the dining room table. She slammed the book closed. There. Out of sight, out of mind. Probably just someone's idea of a joke, anyway.

She took off her coat and kicked her Nikes into a corner. Now, what to have for dinner. She was debating the merits of Pot Noodles versus Sainsbury's Chicken Korma when the doorbell rang. Anne jumped. She wasn't expecting anyone. Not that there was really anyone to expect. She hadn't been in London long enough to make many friends. She closed the fridge and padded over to the door, standing on tiptoe to look through the spyhole.

Oh shit! The doctor. He was looking directly at the spyhole, as if daring her to refuse him entry. She sank down off her toes and held her breath. Go away, you bastard. Ten seconds passed. Twenty. Anne began to hope he actually had gone away when the doorbell rang again, causing her heart to jump in her chest. She took a deep breath and opened the door. "Yes?"

"Hello, Anne. I'd like to speak to you for a minute. May I come in?" He leaned forward, as if expecting immediate acquiescence.

Anne wanted to say no. She was perfectly entitled to say no. But she couldn't bring herself to be that rude. And, she rationalized, it was best to keep things civil between them. He lived right next door. She had to pass him in the hallway. He might be dangerous and she didn't want to set him off. She stepped back and waved him in.

He strode to the center of the room and then stopped, looking around as if searching for something. Anne stayed near the door, leaving it ajar. She watched him warily as he went over to the bookcase by the window and glanced at the volumes on the top shelf.

"You're a computer programmer," he said, nodding at the books.

"Yes."

"It's not a subject I know much about," he said as he moved over to the dining room table and picked up the volume of data processing algorithms. "I prefer studying the human mind to the computerized one. Much more rewarding, don't you think?" He paused, expecting a response, but Anne had stopped listening. Her eyes were fixed on the book in his hands. She held her breath as he turned it over and read the back cover. It seemed to take him forever, but finally he set the book back down on the table. Anne gave such a loud sigh of relief that Dr. Davidson turned and looked at her questioningly.

She pasted what she hoped was a neutral expression on her face. "What can I do for you?"

"It's just a small matter. I was wondering if Jimmy Soames – you met him last week, in my flat – had spoken to you. Contacted you by phone, by mail, by email. Sometime within the last few days."

"No, he hasn't. Why?"

The doctor studied her for several seconds before replying. "He was killed yesterday. Or committed suicide. The police aren't sure yet. The papers gave it a brief coverage. His parents are friends of mine and have asked me to find out what I can about his last days. I haven't seen him for a week, but I was wondering if he had stopped by, perhaps spoken to you in the hall."

"No, I haven't seen him. There's no reason why he would contact me. I barely know the guy." Anne's gaze roamed around the room. She tried to look anywhere but at the book, but it felt like a huge magnet drawing her gaze toward it.

The doctor sauntered over, stopping uncomfortably close to her. Anne found herself face to face with the ducks on his gray silk tie.

"Are you sure?" he asked. "The police have already spoken to me, as Jimmy's doctor. They're looking for people who may have talked to him within the last few days. It wouldn't do to lie to them."

Anne's chin jerked up angrily. "I have no reason to lie to them. Now, if you don't mind, I'm hungry and I'd like to have my dinner."

Dr. Davidson stared down at the top of her head as if trying to read her mind through her skull.

"Of course," he said finally. "So sorry to have disturbed you." His tone managed to be both impeccably polite and completely unapologetic.

After he left Anne shut and bolted the door. She leaned her head against it, her stomach churning like a washing machine on rinse cycle. Taking a deep breath, she went over to the table and opened the book to the page where the letter was. She took it out and stared at the address on the back. Wardour Street, Soho. The epicenter of London's club scene. Ravers, lap dancing, and drugs. A fashionable but skanky area. Anne glanced out the window. Dusk was settling into night. No way was she going to some unfamiliar address in Soho after dark. No, it would have to wait until tomorrow.

Wyndham Prep. Other than the address, it was the only concrete detail in the letter. Dinner temporarily forgotten, she went into the bedroom and dug her laptop out from under the bed. She blew off the dust bunnies which were mating on its surface, plopped it on the duvet and sat cross-legged in front of it. After Windows was up and running she opened the web browser and typed the words 'Wyndham Preparatory' into Google. Only a few entries came up. Most pointed to the same URL: www.wyndhamprep.co.uk. She clicked on the first entry. It was the home page for a boys school called Wyndham Preparatory, located in Kent. Her English geography was still a bit fuzzy, but she was pretty sure that Kent was a county somewhere to the south of London. The web page showed pictures of little white boys ranging in age from about eight to sixteen, all dressed in goofy gray shorts, red blazers, and what looked like red baseball caps. Bizarre. Anne winced at the thought of a boy dressed like that showing up at the junior high school she'd attended in LA's San Fernando Valley. He'd have been torn to pieces – by the girls.

Her mystery note implied that Dr. Davidson had a connection with the school. As a student? She clicked on a link which said 'Alumni'. A box appeared, inviting her to type in a name. A search on 'Davidson' found no matches. Not a student then. Perhaps a teacher? She scrolled back to the home page. The current staff was listed at the bottom of the page – but no Davidson. Possibly the doctor had been on the staff of Wyndham Preparatory at some time in the past, but did she really care? The writer of the anonymous note obviously did, but Anne felt a reluctance to pursue the matter. It felt like someone was trying to make use of her, for their own ends. Probably someone who had a grudge against the doctor. Not that she begrudged them their grudge. Dr. Davidson was certainly the type to create resentment. But still, she didn't like the feeling that someone had volunteered her for the role of pawn in their private chess game. She shut the laptop and shoved it back under the bed. Dinner awaited.

AT 11:30 A.M. on a Monday morning the Central line car was nearly empty. Anne sat back in her seat and absently glanced at the ads pasted on the curved walls of Holborn tube station. Smirnoff had paid for a double-helping of wall space. The ad's elegant model – attired in a dove gray satin gown – eloquently portrayed what the average person looked like after downing lots and lots of vodka.

Anne exited the train at Oxford Circus, hurrying past a street performer who'd brought along his own portable amplifier. Its screeches echoed off the concrete walls of the tube station like a banshee in heat. Pushing through the turnstile, Anne inserted herself into the endless river of humanity which flowed along Oxford Street. Not for the first time, she wished the sidewalks in London came equipped with lane dividers to channel the traffic in one direction. She brought foot traffic to a crashing halt in front of Marks and Spencer, when her legs became entangled by a dog's leash. A bushy Pomeranian chugging along in front of her had attempted a kamikaze dash into an oncoming barrage of baby strollers.

The appearance of Wardour Street came as sweet relief. As most of the crowd kept strictly to Oxford Street, oblivious to its tributaries, Wardour was an oasis of calm by comparison. Anne checked the number painted above the nearest doorway. Ninety-one. Her mystery address wasn't far. Grumpily asserting to herself that she was nobody's pawn, she strode hurriedly down the cracked sidewalk. She was on her lunch hour and was eager to get this excursion over with as quickly as possible.

She slowed. 113, 115 . . . there. 116. Other side of the street. An anonymous blue door, bordered by a Vodafone shop on one side and a bar called 'Xctasy' on the other. Anne snorted at the bar owner's lack of originality and ran her gaze up the building. The ground floor was strictly business, but it looked like the upper levels of the four-storey structure held living quarters. Curtains hung in the dusty windows, the unmistakable screams of a Jerry Springer audience blared out into the street.

THE DOOR OF Flat B was ajar. Anne hesitated on the narrow landing. The ground floor entrance had also been unlocked and unattended. Such things were unheard of in security-conscious London. She glanced up at the ceiling, half-expecting to find video cameras filming someone's idea of an elaborate practical joke. Dusty cobwebs were in evidence, but no cameras.

Her timid knock on the door barely dented the silence. She forced out a more assertive rap with her knuckles. Nothing. Nudging the groaning door open wider, she edged her head into the room. A studio, by the look of it. A grubby toilet was partially concealed behind a crude pasteboard partition, but otherwise the entire flat could be seen from the front door. An unmade bed, twisted sheets dragging on the floor, was parked under a lurid Harley-Davidson poster. A pyramid of Budweiser cans was stacked in one corner like an unholy Christmas tree.

Anne jumped as the door to Flat A below her suddenly banged open. She peered cautiously over the banister, but Flat A's tenant had already vanished out into the street.

She slunk back into the flat and turned full circle. Now that she had reached her goal she realized that she had no idea what to do next. She executed another slow circle, just to feel productive. It was obvious, now that she'd seen the place, why no one had bothered to lock up. There was nothing here to steal. Even junkies would turn their nose up at the offerings.

A rickety card table attracted her gaze – and her nose. The table was piled high with empty takeaway cartons, pizza boxes, and more beer cans. Cigarettes smoked down to the tiniest of stubs overflowed cheap tin ashtrays. Jumbled in with the trash were several piles of paper. Anne gingerly picked through one, half expecting a mouse and cockroach duo to leap out and regale her with the vermin version of 'Life is a Cabaret, Old Chum'.

Electric bills, stamped with a big red 'Overdue', right in the center. Takeaway menus from The House of Balti and Chang's Chinese Garden. Anne lifted an empty Pizza Hut box, revealing another stack of papers – and a hypodermic needle, its tip rusty red. She jumped back as if bitten. Using the pizza box, she carefully rolled the needle off the papers. More overdue bills, this time from Orange, a mobile phone company. The name on the account was Rick Billingsley. Anne chewed on her lower lip. She'd seen that name somewhere. She tugged on her hair in frustration, but it refused to come to her.

Shaking a smattering of crumbs off the phone bill, she folded it and tucked it in the pocket of her jeans. She rifled quickly through the rest of the stack. Bills, bills, more menus . . . an envelope from Quick Snaps. She slid the photos out, standard four-by-six inch prints. The top one showed a group of men in paper hats, all holding beer bottles. Some kind of party. The next was – oh my. Apparently the party was of the bachelor persuasion. Anne rapidly skipped to the next one, her eyes squinted nearly shut. Okay, this one wasn't so bad. She peered at it. Three men. The one on the left, a clean-shaven black guy wearing a suit and tie, looked the most respectable. The white guy in the middle, staring vacantly at the camera, was . . . hey! Jimmy! Anne looked closer. The man was wearing what looked like a woman's flannel nightgown, and he was definitely Jimmy Soames. Standing a full head shorter than the other two, he looked fragile and rather lost. The third man was tall and tanned, with a scraggly goatee and a silver earring dangling almost to his shoulder. He looked like an amateur actor appearing in a roadshow version of 'The Pirates of Penzance' (tickets available now at the Bournemouth Senior Centre, only two pounds for you over Sixty-Fives).

Anne flipped the photo over. No helpful names or dates. No other pictures of Jimmy in the stack. She tucked the rest of the photos back into their envelope, cramming the one of Jimmy in her pocket.

BACK AT HER desk, Anne idly scrolled through cnn.com. Nick was off at some database seminar, so she had the small office to herself. She stretched her legs out luxuriously. Without Nick the tiny space seemed more than ample. When he was in residence his manic energy and non-stop fidgeting made her feel she was sharing the room with a swarm of RedBull-swigging bumblebees.

She yawned. Amazing how international news headlines could be both horrific and soporific. She switched over to the home page for the London Times, taking an unenthusiastic bite out of an egg salad sandwich. She scrolled past the headlines down to the local news, hoping for a bit of entertaining fluff. 'Poodle Goes on Hunger Strike, Prefers Death to Baby-Blue Doggie Sweater Knitted By Owner – Mrs. Maise Poppington of Upper-Bottoms-By-The-Sea, Sussex'. Something like that. A blurb at the bottom of the page caught her eye: 'Suspect in Soames Murder Released'. Two short paragraphs followed:

'Rick Billingsley was released by the Metropolitan Police today. Billingsley is a suspect in the murder of The Honorable James Soames, whose body was recovered from the Thames ten days ago. When asked why Billingsley was released, a police spokesman replied that there was not sufficient evidence to hold him. Billingsley has been asked not to leave London. In a surprise announcement, Dr. John Davidson, Mr. Soames' psychiatrist, told the press that he had reason to believe Daniel Soames, brother of the deceased, was involved in the crime. Daniel Soames could not be reached for comment.'

Huh. Anne stared thoughtfully at the screen. Rick Billingsley. The occupant of the flat on Wardour Street. And Dr. Davidson. Her neighbor was apparently determined to involve himself in the matter.

But why? She'd have thought it better for his psychiatric practice to stay well clear of a police investigation. Negative publicity and all that. Unless . . . that anonymous note she'd received. It had clearly been written by someone with a grudge against the doctor. If the writer of the note was trying to point a finger at the doctor, perhaps frame him for Jimmy's murder, then the doctor's announcement to the press might simply be self-defense. Pointing the finger at someone else. Maybe this Daniel Soames inherited money on his brother's death. Of course, if Daniel Soames' motive was that obvious then the police would already have considered him a suspect. Maybe Dr. Davidson was just feeling desperate.

Anne mulled this over. If she had an anonymous enemy who was trying to frame her for murder she'd be feeling desperate too. She felt a bit sorry for the doctor. Hard to believe, but true.

She dug into her purse. From an inside zippered pocket she pulled out the anonymous note. She'd been carrying it around with her all week, uncertain what to do with it. Now she had an idea. The note was handwritten. The writer obviously knew the doctor, so it was possible that Dr. Davidson might recognize the handwriting.

She debated with herself for ten minutes before finally deciding. She opened Google and typed the words: 'John Davidson', 'psychiatrist', and 'London' into the search engine. The search returned two entries, both with the same URL. She clicked on the top one. Yep. He had his own web page, or rather his practice did. Three names popped up, all psychiatrists, and a small picture of a white-haired gentleman whose expression said: 'I care about *you*, not your money'. The address listed was Austin Friars House. Anne wasn't familiar with the building, but a quick check of the London map she kept in her desk revealed an Austin Friars street only a few blocks from her office. The street name sounded strange to her American ears. The Friars were probably some group of monks who had lived in the area centuries ago. The 'Austin' made her think of Texas, but somehow she doubted that the brothers had hailed from the Lone Star state.

The web page didn't divulge much more information, just an address, a phone number and office hours. Hyperlinks underlined the name of each psychiatrist. Anne clicked on the link under 'Dr. John Davidson'.

The resulting web page contained only a few lines. It informed her that the doctor had studied at Cambridge, that he had been practicing psychiatry for twenty years, and that he had been at the Austin Friars Psychiatric Clinic for the last seven.

Anne glanced at the clock on the bottom of her screen. 2:30. She had a meeting at 4:00. If she hurried she'd be back in time. She logged off the computer and shrugged on her parka.

A gust of air whooshed at her as she left her office building. It had that just-scrubbed feeling present after a heavy rainfall. Anne cut across Finsbury Road and through the park surrounding the bowling green in the middle of the square. No bowlers, as usual. The benches around the green were also deserted, the decayed remains of fallen maple leaves plastering their seats. It was too cold to dine out al fresco, though normally a few brave souls could be found eating their Pret a Manger sandwiches in the square.

Anne turned onto one of the main thoroughfares of the City, a wide street called London Wall. Sections of a roman-built wall, two-thousand years old, lay scattered around the area, clashing with the shiny glass and steel of modern skyscrapers. Black cabs rushed by, nearly knocking down stock traders as they charged across the street, single-mindedly discussing deals while ignoring traffic.

Anne dodged around a group of suits spilling out of the elaborate Victorian façade of the Rose and Crown pub and caught sight of a street marked Austin Friars. It was narrow, little more than an alleyway. Austin Friars House rose imposingly in front of her. The four-story building of gray stone had lifesize female figures carved above the windows, holding what looked like fruit baskets on their heads – Carmen Miranda as depicted by Michelangelo.

Anne hesitated. Okay, she was here. Now what? Pedestrians pushed past her on the sidewalk. She stepped into a doorway to get out of shoving range and stood there for a few minutes, watching people go in and out of Austin Friars House. A UPS delivery man held the door open for a red-haired woman in an Armani suit. The woman paused on the steps of the building and turned to talk to the man who had followed her out. His grey suit was impeccably tailored, his white-blond hair incandescent in the February sunshine. Dr. Davidson.

Anne watched the doctor shake hands with the woman and head off toward London Wall. It was now or never. She slipped out of the doorway and hurried after him.

"Excuse me."

The doctor kept walking.

She tried again. "Dr. Davidson."

He halted, a frown narrowing his transparent blue eyes. "Miss Lambert. This is unexpected." He waited, his expression shifting to blandly unhelpful.

Anne repressed the urge to kick him. "I have something I'd like to discuss with you," she forced out through gritted teeth. "Not here," she added as a passing pedestrian bumped her shoulder. "Could we go up to your office for a few minutes?"

THE PRE-WWII LIFT clunked to a halt on the second floor. Anne followed the doctor down a carpeted hallway toward a dusty ficus tree. A bronze plaque on the wall announced that this was indeed the Austin Friars Psychiatric Clinic. The clinic's door opened into a waiting room decorated in soothing tones of blue and mauve. No patients sat in the slip-covered armchairs. Anne wondered if this was just a lunchtime phenomenon, or if it indicated the state of the business. A reception desk to her left was empty. As the doctor paused at the desk and flipped through a pile of mail in the inbox a clink of dishes came from a room just off the waiting area. An elderly woman in a gray tweed suit and pearls emerged carrying a mug of coffee. The steam wafted over to Anne. Hazelnut Mocha.

The woman smiled at Dr. Davidson. "Back so soon doctor?"

"Yes Mrs. Reed. Dining out lost its appeal. Would you call The Gates of Siam and order me some Pad Thai?"

"Certainly. Anything for the young lady?" asked the receptionist, gazing curiously at Anne.

"No thanks," Anne said politely.

"We'll be in my office," said the doctor, putting one hand on the small of Anne's back. Her back muscles went rigid at his touch and she jerked away from him.

The doctor looked vaguely amused, but didn't respond. The room he led Anne into was large and ornate, its high ceiling festooned with plaster rosettes. The walls were painted a delicate shade of yellow, the furniture a Scandinavian style in pale blond wood. The effect whispered of wealth and status. It didn't seem like a room designed to inspire troubled patients to unburden themselves. Instead, it seemed designed to intimidate. Dr. Davidson put a hand on her shoulder and pressed her down into an armchair covered in a pale yellow silk jacquard. Anne ran a finger along the smooth fabric and did a quick mental survey of her jeans for evidence of the tomato sauce from last night's spaghetti dinner. As far as she knew the chair was not in any danger.

The doctor set his mail down on a sculpted pine desk, which looked more like art than furniture, and leaned against it. He folded his arms and stared down at Anne in a pose so reminiscent of a cartoon villain that she couldn't help herself. She giggled.

"Not many people find me amusing," he said, not angrily, but as if he had met a new and strange personality type which didn't exist in his psychiatry manuals. "Care to tell me what's so funny?"

"No," coughed Anne, glancing around the room to distract herself. The curtains flowing down from the double-height windows were the same expensive silk she was sitting on. A Persian rug in an intricate pattern of pale rose lay under her feet. No office equipment anywhere. No computer on the desk, nothing at all on its varnished surface except for a blank pad of writing paper and a single ballpoint pen.

"Does the room meet with your approval?" asked the doctor, a smug note in his voice.

"It's very elegant, though maybe a trifle feminine."

"I had a decorator do it," said the doctor, not rising to the bait. "She's one of the best in London. She did the recent renovation of the estate belonging to Princess Michael of Kent." He paused so that Anne could make the requisite noises of awe. When she just stared at him he continued. "Jimmy used to come here for his weekly sessions. It seems strange that he's not around anymore. I've been treating him for years. He was annoying, but I guess I'd gotten used to seeing him."

As well as used to being paid by him, Anne thought. Interior design by Princess Michael of Kent's decorator didn't come cheap.

"Have you been following Jimmy's murder in the papers?" asked the doctor. "The Times had a short article on it in the morning edition."

"Yes, I saw it," replied Anne. She dug into her purse and pulled out the anonymous note. She nervously tapped it with her finger. "This . . . well, I'm not sure what this is, exactly. It might be relevant to the article. Anyway, I thought you should see it." She handed over the note.

The doctor frowned at her, then glanced at the address scrawled on the back of the note. He shrugged and turned the sheet over.

Anne was watching him closely, and she could have sworn something flickered across his usually immobile face. The drawbridge had been raised, and the guards posted on the Keep. He recognized the handwriting. She was sure of it.

"Where did you get this?" he asked.

"It was left in my mailbox at the Barbican. It seems, well, it seems to refer to you. I felt you had a right to see it. It looks like you have an enemy." Which was hardly surprising, Anne thought snippily. A person as unpleasant as the doctor undoubtedly had enough enemies to fill Hyde Park.

The doctor didn't respond.

"Do you have any idea who it might be?" Anne prompted.

"No", snapped the doctor. "It mentions Wyndham Preparatory, a boys school in Kent I used to work at, many years ago. If I had to guess, I'd say this is from one of those obnoxious little boys, now an obnoxious little man. There were hundreds of the brats. Obviously, one of them has held onto a childish grudge against me. Something trivial happened to him twenty years ago, he blames me for it, and now he's writing anonymous notes to make himself feel important. Undoubtedly someone with insecurity issues, since he's writing notes rather than approaching me face to face." He crumpled the note and dropped it in the wastebasket next to his desk. "Thank you for bringing this to my attention. Now, if you'll excuse me, I need to prepare for my next appointment."

Chapter Three

IT WAS PITCH black inside her flat when Anne got home from work that evening. Heavy rain clouds were hovering over the city, blotting out the moon and giving the streetlights more work than they could handle. Anne turned on every light in her flat and closed the drapes. Once she had changed into her pink bathrobe and cranked up the radiator things felt downright cozy. Let the heavens open. She had macaroni and cheese in the cupboard and 'Friends' on TV.

Before going to bed that night Anne wrote down, word for word, the contents of the anonymous note which now resided at the bottom of Dr. Davidson's wastebasket. She had no trouble remembering its few short lines. She tucked this into an envelope, together with the mobile phone bill and the photo of Jimmy Soames she'd found in Rick Billingsley's flat. She labeled the envelope 'Jimmy' and stuck it into an accordion file which held her tax forms. There. All neatly filed away, ready to be forgotten. She breathed a sigh of relief, content that she'd done her duty. She chucked the accordion file into the darkest corner of her bedroom closet.

✦ ✦ ✦ ✦

ANNE HUMMED 'THE Anvil Song' from Il Trovatore as she threaded her way through the Barbican's concrete walkways. The morning rush hour was in full force as she emerged into the throng of pedestrians and black cabs pulsing down London Wall, but even the packed sidewalks and overcast sky couldn't dent her mood. She felt as if a heavy knapsack had been lifted from her shoulders. The police knew about Rick Billingsley, and Dr. Davidson knew about the anonymous note. Jimmy's murder was being investigated . . . everyone knew everything they were supposed to know, and she no longer felt the weight of responsibility which the anonymous note writer had tried to dump on her. Life was good, and, more importantly, back to normal.

At the intersection of London Wall and Moorgate the light changed to red, backing pedestrian traffic up into a tight knot. Anne teetered on the curb, trying not to get pushed into the street by the mass of bodies behind her. When the light changed the green Walk signal registered in her mind, but the fact that the other pedestrians were leaping back onto the curb did not. She was halfway across the street when the midnight blue Mercedes hit her from the side.

IT WAS DARK when she woke. Anne tried to raise her head, gasping when a stabbing pain shot through her left eye. She shut both eyes tightly and tried to breath through the pain, the way her track coach had taught her in college. It didn't help much with the pain, but it calmed her a bit. She tried an exploratory sniff. Rubbing alcohol. It smelled like a doctor's office. The room she was in was quiet. She could hear voices, but they were a long way off. She slowly opened her eyes and tried to focus, careful not to move her head. Two dark, rectangular objects hovered in front of her, high up on a white wall, near the ceiling. She squinted at them. Their edges were fuzzy. Suddenly one of them blinked out of existence for a moment, then reappeared. Anne realized what she was looking at. It was a television set, mounted up on the wall. But two televisions that close to each other made no sense. Of course. She had double vision. Weird. She'd never had a head injury before. It was unsettling.

She tried glancing to the left and right without turning her head, but couldn't see much. She was covered with a sheet and a lightweight plaid blanket. It was a hospital bed. She was in a hospital. Again weird. She'd never been in a hospital before, if you didn't count the trips to the emergency room as a kid. Four broken bones in four years. It was a family record. She could now add a fifth bone to the list. Her left wrist was broken. She had broken her right wrist falling out of a tree when she was eleven. Now she had a matching set. The feeling was exactly the same. That strange ache, and an inability to move her fingers. The plaster cast on her arm reached from wrist to elbow. She cautiously wiggled other body parts. To her great relief her toes moved on command. She wasn't paralyzed.

Her right side was sore – she probably had some spectacular bruises – but on the whole she wasn't in bad shape. She was tired and dizzy, but her thinking wasn't clouded, so the head injury couldn't be too severe. In fact, she could remember what had happened – a car had hit her. Odd. She thought accident victims generally couldn't remember the accident. The idea that it might not be an accident tried to sneak into her thoughts, but she pushed it away. Her mind played hide and seek with the idea until she fell asleep again.

WHEN SHE WOKE there were voices in the room. She opened her eyes, and then shut them again, wincing at the glare. "I'll turn off the lights," someone said. She tried again, squinting warily. That was better. It was daytime. Sunlight slanted into the room from a window to her left, creating a little pool of warmth on her toes. She wriggled them and tried to focus on the TV in front of her. Much better. Its edges were still fuzzy, but only one TV appeared on the wall this time, not two. A woman's face floated above her.

"Hello Anne. I'm Dr. Millar. You're in St. Bartholomew's Hospital. You look much improved today. I'm just going to do a few quick tests." She shone a light into Anne's eyes. "Look up please. Good. Now left. Right. Down. Good. How many fingers am I holding up?

And now? Good. No double vision. You have a concussion, but it's not serious."

"Things look fuzzy," said Anne.

"Yes. That will disappear in a day or two. You may have head-aches for a while. If they persist for more than two weeks come see me. I've scheduled a follow-up appointment anyway, for next Tuesday."

"Are you sure my head's okay?"

"Yes. We did a full CAT scan, as well as x-rays of your skull and spinal column. You were lucky. It could have been a lot worse. You have a broken left wrist, as you've no doubt noticed. No other injuries except some bruising. Now, the police are here. They need to talk to you. I'm just going to raise you up a bit."

Anne heard a whirring noise and the top half of the bed slanted upward until she was in a half-sitting, half-lying down position. It was better than lying flat on her back while strangers hovered over her, but she still felt awkward. She pulled the blanket up to her neck and crossed her right arm over her chest. The doctor bustled out and two people stepped forward, a man and a woman. The woman had a short gray bob and wore a well-cut navy suit. The man was more casually dressed in a shirt and khakis.

"Miss Lambert, I'm Inspector Beckett, and this is DC Singh." The woman held up a small leather folder containing her ID. Anne squinted at it, but her eyesight was too fuzzy to make out the picture. She nodded anyway.

"We need to ask you a few questions about the accident. Do you remember what happened?"

"Yes. I was walking to work along London Wall and I got hit by a car."

"You were hit at the corner of London Wall and Moorgate. Is that the route you usually take to work?"

"Yes." Anne noticed that DC Singh had taken out a worn green notebook and was diligently writing in it.

"Did you see the car that hit you?"

"No, not really. All I remember is a brief flash of something large and dark coming at me from my right side."

"Has anyone threatened you recently?"

Anne's mouth dropped open in surprise. Both officers were watching her closely. Her grip on the hospital blanket tightened. "No," she said finally. "Why?"

"There are indications that this wasn't an accident. We believe the driver of the car may have hit you deliberately."

Anne grew cold. She closed her eyes. The silence stretched as the officers waited for her to respond. A confusing storm of thoughts about Jimmy Soames, Dr. Davidson, Rick Billingsley, and the anonymous note whirled through her head. She didn't know what to say or where to start, so she said nothing.

"Do you know of anyone who would want to hurt or even kill you?" asked the inspector. "Husband, boyfriend, ex-boyfriends?"

"I . . . No," said Anne quietly.

"There were plenty of witnesses to the accident. Pulling a stunt like this during rush hour – it was almost as if he wanted an audience. Several witnesses agreed that the car was a dark blue Mercedes four-door. The car had tinted windows, but two witnesses swear that the driver was a man, possibly with blond or light brown hair. And we were even more fortunate. One gentleman chased the car on foot, and when it was caught in traffic 50 yards down Moorgate he noted down the license number. The car belongs to a Mr. Daniel Soames. Do you know Mr. Soames?"

"I know a Jimmy Soames. Well, I don't really know him. I met him once when he came to visit my neighbor. He died a week ago. It was in the papers."

"Yes, we know. The case is still open. Quite a coincidence, don't you think. Jimmy Soames dies and a week later someone in his brother's car runs you down."

Anne glanced up at her. "Then you don't think it was Daniel Soames driving the car?"

"We don't know. We talked to him yesterday morning, a few hours after the accident. He claims he was at home at the time it happened, about 8:30 a.m. He says that as far as he knows his car was in the underground parking garage beneath his residence. He walks to work, so he doesn't use the car on weekdays. He claims he didn't use it at all yesterday. He took us down to his parking spot, and the car was there. We've impounded it. So, there are two conclusions we can make. Either Mr. Soames is lying, or someone borrowed his Mercedes, ran you down, and then returned the car to its parking place."

The Inspector paused and DC Singh looked up from his notebook. "This neighbor who Jimmy Soames visited, what is his name?" he asked.

"Dr. Davidson. John Davidson. He lives next door to me in the Barbican. In Andrewes House."

The Inspector turned to DC Singh. "Davidson. That name sounds familiar."

"Yes. He was questioned about the Jimmy Soames death." DC Singh flipped back through his notebook. "Not as a suspect, but because he was treating the deceased. He's a psychiatrist."

The Inspector frowned, absentmindedly twisting the thin gold necklace which hung down over her jacket. "Strange that he would have patients visiting him at home. Unless his practice is located in his flat." She looked questioningly at the constable.

"No, I don't think so." DC Singh flipped through more pages. "I have the address somewhere . . . ah, here it is. Austin Friars House. It's in the City, just off Old Broad street. Davidson is one of three psychiatrists at the Austin Friars Psychiatric Clinic."

"What was he treating Jimmy Soames for?" asked the Inspector.

"Alcoholism."

"I'd like to talk to this Dr. Davidson," said Inspector Beckett to the constable. "Who did the original interview?"

"DI Lawson, Snow Hill Division."

"Right. We'll talk to him too." She handed Anne a business card. "My number's on here. Call me if anything else occurs to you," she said pointedly.

They left Anne staring down at the blurry card in her hand. She felt like a six-year old with a skinned knee who was getting zero sympathy from Mommy and Daddy. She was just entering self-pity city when she nodded off.

ANNE'S EYES SNAPPED open. She couldn't remember where she was. She was in bed, but instead of her comfy – if not always freshly laundered – duvet a thin, well-worn plaid blanket covered her. Then a piece in her brain seemed to shift. Oh, right. Hospital. She closed her left eye, then the right. Much better. The fuzziness was gone. She gingerly felt her head. A bump the size of an ostrich egg swelled above her right ear. She pushed on it and stars suddenly appeared, streaking across her vision. Ok. That was enough exploration. If other bumps had sprouted on her head she didn't want to know about them.

Something had woken her up. Some noise. She was sure of it. She'd been dreaming about the Muppets. Kermit the Frog was hatching a plan for world domination, with Miss Piggy coordinating the air raids, when blam – she was wide awake. She turned her head carefully to the left. Nothing there. Just an empty room with sunshine coming in through the partially open window. The industrial-grade curtains were billowing in the breeze. London appeared to be having a freak spell of good weather. And here she was stuck in bed. Maybe they'd let her go home today. Not that she felt up to any outdoor activities. She yawned and turned her head to the right.

"Good Morning."

Dr. Davidson was sitting in a chair next to her bed, hands folded in his lap, observing her calmly. A bunch of white carnations tied with a grosgrain ribbon lay on the nightstand.

"I just stopped by to see how you were," he said, running a hand down his gray silk tie. Tiny red horses were racing each other across it.

"How did you know I was here?" croaked Anne, staring at him like a fieldmouse about to become a snake snack.

"Your accident was in The Evening Standard." He handed her a folded newspaper. "You can keep it. Just think of it as a souvenir." There was an odd overtone to this last remark which Anne couldn't place. Threat? Humor? It was impossible to say.

She opened the paper, which was folded at page twenty-three. She scanned the page for her name and found it at the bottom in a tiny paragraph. No picture. The accident was described as a hit-and-run, and witnesses were encouraged to contact the City of London Police, Bishopsgate Division. It mentioned that she'd been taken to St. Bartholomew's Hospital, but no other details were given.

Anne re-folded the paper and ran her fingers along the crease, back and forth until they were black with newsprint. Maybe if she ignored him he would go away. Immature, true, but her post-concussion brain seemed to be stuck in six-year old mode. She was tempted to close her eyes and pretend to fall asleep, but rejected the idea as just too creepy. Being in the same room with him was unpleasant enough. Being in the same room with him with her eyes closed was not to be contemplated.

"Has Daniel been to visit you?" asked the doctor, breaking the awkward silence.

"Pardon?" asked Anne in surprise.

"Daniel Soames. Jimmy's brother. He was the one who hit you."

"Oh, right. The police told me. No, he hasn't been here. The police said it's possible it wasn't him. It was his car, but he may not have been driving it."

"Oh, I expect he was driving it all right," replied the doctor in his confident voice. "Either him or that idiot Billingsley."

"Who?" asked Anne sharply.

"Friend of Daniel's. Always hanging around, touching Daniel up for money. Stays at his flat, borrows his car. According to Jimmy the Soames family tried to pay him off once – stay away from our son and we'll hand you a nice fat wad of cash. Didn't work. Little Daniel's too fond of his cocaine, and Billingsley is his supplier."

"You seem to know a lot about the Soames family's private affairs," said Anne.

"Yes, well, these things come up in therapy. Family is always the main topic of discussion."

"I'm sure that's true, but aren't these things confidential? I mean, should you be telling me this stuff?"

The doctor was studying his manicured fingernails. "The patient is dead," he said calmly. "I doubt that his ghost is bothered by such technicalities."

Anne shivered. The temperature in the room seemed to drop sharply. She pulled the thin blanket up higher over her shoulders. She was about to muster the courage to ask the doctor to leave when he suddenly picked up the bunch of carnations and stood up.

"These reminded me of you," he said, pulling a white petal off and shredding it between his thumb and forefinger. He laid the flowers on the bed and left.

Chapter Four

A NNE SAT AT her desk, chin in hand, watching the rain run down the window in tiny rivers which spilled off the window ledge into a pot of blue hyacinths. It was the first week in March, and hints of spring were evident all over London. Mostly it was daffodils. They had sprung up overnight in flower boxes and planters. Tower Hill was a yellow carpet of daffodils trying to hold up their heads in the rain. Britannic House, the nineteenth century building where Anne worked, had gone with hyacinths instead, their blue petals glowing against the white stone of the building.

Anne had been back to work for a week now. Her left hand was still in its plaster cast, which made typing code difficult. Like all programmers she was a fast typist, and the one-fingered approach she was temporarily reduced to was making her irritable.

"Damn it!" Anne pounded on the backspace key, erasing the gibberish she had just typed.

"Dude, that's gotta be annoying," said Nick, his fingers flying over the keyboard in his lap. He had his feet up on his desk, mud dripping from his Pumas onto the new technical documentation from Barclay's. "If I had one hand in a cast I think I'd just take a long vacation. I mean, how can you work?"

"I can work," replied Anne through gritted teeth. "I'm just doing it a bit more slowly than usual. And besides, programming is more about thinking than typing anyway."

"Yeah, but sooner or later you have to type your thoughts into the computer. What you need is a direct brain-to-PC hookup. Like a broadband cable with nerves on one end and wires on the other. Dude, that would be so cool!"

Anne glared at him, which had no effect whatsoever. It was impossible to squelch Nick. He was the Energizer Bunny of cheerfulness. Normally Anne found his unflagging optimism endearing, but there were times when a girl was just entitled to be in a bad mood. She was dredging her brain for a scathing retort that even Nick couldn't ignore, when she was interrupted by Lindsey's sudden appearance in the doorway.

"Hi guys," said the receptionist. "Anne, there's a gentleman here to see you." Lindsey's nose twitched on 'gentleman' as if she had gotten a whiff of sour milk.

Anne stood up, bruised ribs creaking, and followed Lindsey as she glided down the hall. Lindsey's outfit for the day was a stunning jade green silk dress paired with towering black patent leather heels. Anne had once seen her walking to work in those same shoes, negotiating London's crowded, scaffold-covered, potholed streets as if she were headed down the red carpet on Oscar night. Anne knew she herself would be lucky to just stand up in shoes like those without breaking her ankle.

"I hope this guy isn't a friend of yours," Lindsey said over her shoulder, "because he's very creepy. Plus his nose seems to be over-indulged, if you know what I mean."

"What?" asked Anne, baffled by this last remark.

"Coke," said Lindsey, making sniff-sniff noises.

As they emerged into the reception area a man Anne had never seen before stepped forward. Since he was staring avidly at Lindsey Anne had a chance to study him. He was of medium height, on the thin side, with light brown hair and gray eyes which looked familiar for some reason. He wore a well-tailored dark blue suit which just screamed Boy Trader. Every young male stockbroker in the City had the same suit. She looked carefully at his nose. Yes, it did seem a bit red and runny.

"This is Anne Lambert," said Lindsey, barricading herself behind her desk and ignoring his stares. Since Lindsey had years of experience ignoring gawping males he soon had to admit defeat. He turned to Anne.

"I'm Daniel Soames," he announced in a high-pitched voice so nasal it verged on whiny. He didn't offer his hand. "I just wanted to see for myself that you were okay, and to repeat that I was not the one driving my car when it hit you."

Anne noticed Lindsey's head snap up at this. She hadn't said much about the accident to the people in the office, only mentioning that it had been a hit-and-run.

"Yes," said Anne cautiously. "The police told me it was a possibility that your car had been stolen and then returned."

"It's not a possibility, it's the truth," whined Daniel so petulantly that Anne thought he was going to stamp his feet and launch into a full-scale temper tantrum.

"Okay, it's the truth," Anne replied in her best lets-humor-the-lunatic voice. "Well, I appreciate your coming here to check on me, but as you can see, I'm fine. Now, if you'll excuse me I need to get back to work." She turned to go but was startled to find herself pulled up short. Daniel had grabbed her arm.

"You don't understand. I came here to get you. You need to come to the police station with me. It's over on Bishopsgate." He stopped speaking abruptly, as if that was the end of the matter, and started yanking Anne toward the door. Anne dug her heels in and leaned away from him, looking toward the reception desk for help. Lindsey was already on the case. She dialed building security, and for good measure called Nick as well.

"Nick, come to reception please. Don't ask me why silly boy. Just

THE DANGER NEXT DOOR

get up here." Lindsey dashed out from behind her desk and planted herself in front of the door.

Daniel looked taken aback by this and came to a halt, dropping Anne's arm. Anne was tempted to hit him with her other arm – the one with the plaster cast – but was afraid she'd do more damage to her broken wrist than to him.

Nick rushed in. "What's going on?" he asked, looking like an eager but confused puppy.

"Nick, hit him," commanded Lindsey, pointing imperiously at Daniel Soames.

"Uh, okay," said Nick.

"Whoa, wait a minute!" said Daniel, jumping backwards. "There's no need for that. We're just going to the police station."

"Anne's not going anywhere with you," said Lindsey.

"But she has to," whined Daniel. "The police have my car and I want it back. Plus, they think I ran her down, which I didn't. I don't even know her. She has to tell the police that I didn't hit her."

"I can't do that," said Anne. "I don't know who hit me. I didn't even see the car, much less the driver."

"But . . ." began Daniel.

"Stop. No more of this. You're leaving. Now." Lindsey stepped aside and pointed at the door like a traffic cop who was having a really bad day.

Daniel looked for a moment like he was going to argue the point again, but finally he slumped in defeat and slunk out the door, letting it bang behind him.

"Well!" exclaimed Lindsey. "What an unpleasant person." She politely avoided looking at Anne as she took her place behind the reception desk again. Nick, however, was not so circumspect.

"What the heck was that about?" he asked.

"That was Daniel Soames," answered Anne. "It was his car that ran me down, but like he said, the police can't prove that he was driving it."

"He seems like a real jerk either way," said Nick. "If he shows up again you just let me know. I'll teach him a lesson." He threw a vigorous punch at the air, scrawny arms quivering. Lindsey rolled her eyes.

"Yes junior, you're very brave. Now, be a good boy and go back to work."

"Okay," said Nick cheerfully. He disappeared down the hall, throwing a ferocious punch at a ficus tree along the way. The ficus looked unimpressed.

Lindsey was eyeing Anne speculatively. "I don't want to pry," she began, "but is there something you'd like to talk about? It's almost noon. We could grab some lunch. The Tandoori place on Moorgate is having a two-for-one special."

Anne appreciated the significance of the offer. Lindsey's lunch hour was invariably filled with adoring guys treating her to three-course meals at Chez Gerard. Chatting with a co-worker over chicken tikka was definitely slumming.

"That's really nice of you," she began, "but I'm just not ready . . ."

"Not ready to talk about it?" asked Lindsey. "Absolutely not a problem. Just remember that I'll be happy to listen if you change your mind. Now," she said as she picked up the phone, "I'm going to give building security a piece of my mind. What good are they if they don't come when you call them?"

Chapter Five

F AT, APPARENTLY, WAS in. Anne squinched her nose up in distaste as she contemplated the latest addition to the Tate Modern's collection of Really Weird Stuff. She decided that Joseph Beuys was not one of her favorite artists, though it seemed that many of the over-dressed art lovers around her disagreed.

"The felt wraps around the fat like a lover's embrace," said a woman in a pink-sequined cocktail dress, her red fingernails pointing provocatively at a splodgy sculpture which looked ready to fall off its pedestal in greasy chunks.

"Please," said the man next to her. "It looks more like my obese Aunt Millicent wrapped in her felt overcoat. Let's head over to the buffet. I hear Flying Chef is catering. They did baked king prawns at the Courtauld Institute which were to die for."

Anne moved closer to read the plaque under the disintegrating sculpture, nearly bumping heads with a fellow exhibit attendee.

"Sorry. I didn't see you," she said.

"No, my fault entirely." A pair of boyish blue eyes twinkled at her. "I was so enthralled by the sight of such elegance that I lost control." He shoved a thatch of black hair out of his eyes and waved a hand in the air, outlining the shape of the sculpture.

Anne looked at him doubtfully. "Really?" she said, wondering if he was entirely sane.

He grinned at her. "No, not really. Beuys has some interesting themes, but his execution leaves a lot to be desired. I'm much more fond of Anselm Kiefer myself. Do you know his work?"

"I'm afraid not," said Anne apologetically.

"No reason you should. No reason at all. I keep forgetting not everyone is an art geek like myself. I'm a student at the Royal College of Art. Jason Gilbert."

Anne shook the hand he held out, predisposed to like him because he was one of the few people at the exhibit who was casually dressed. Besides herself, of course. Their T-shirts and jeans stood out in the sea of sequins and tuxedos like two sparrows thrown in with a passel of peacocks.

"And you are?" asked Jason.

"Anne. *Not* a student at the Royal College of Art."

"Well, then I certainly shouldn't be seen talking to you." His blue eyes pretended to scan the crowd, searching for a more profitable target to chat up, before zeroing back in on her. "Sorry. There I go again. My sister is constantly reminding me not to tease people so much. Especially complete strangers. But then, we're not strangers. We've bonded over Beuys. Would you like a prawn?"

"Wha. . ." Anne was a bit slow making the leap from Beuys to prawns, partly because she had decided that Jason was quite attractive, in a twenty-something sort of way. She had been trying to guess his age, finally settling on twenty-five. Which was way too young. She preferred guys in her own age group, somewhere in their thirties. Guys still in their twenties generally had no depth. They were all penis and ego.

"Can I get you something from the buffet?" Jason added by way of clarification.

"Oh. I see. Why don't I come with you."

They threaded their way through the crowd and attached themselves to the end of the buffet queue. Jason grabbed a plate and began piling on the prawns, not to mention the baby roast potatoes, the mini-quiches oozing edam, and the asparagus wrapped in Prosciutto. Anne skipped the prawns, but took a sample of everything else. She was tempted to squeeze in the crème brulee when they arrived at the dessert section, but there was no room left on her plate. A return trip was definitely in order she decided, eyeing the Death By Chocolate and a Pavlova so light and fluffy it looked ready to float right out of its bowl.

Jealously guarding their full plates from the jostling crowd, they made their way to the central hall of the museum. Scores of round tables covered in white sheeting had been set up in this cavernous space – the former heart of the Bankside power station. The power station had started its transformation into the Tate Museum of Modern Art in 1995. A giant crane formerly used for hauling machinery was still visible high above their heads. Art exhibit chit-chat echoed off the steel walls. They were hunting for an empty table when Jason turned to her.

"Some guy is waving at you," he said, sounding a bit miffed at this development.

Anne followed Jason's pointing champagne glass. The man wasn't hard to spot, being one of the few men in the museum not dressed in a tuxedo. Dr. Davidson was wearing his usual elegant gray suit, his transparent blond hair slicked back from his forehead. The change in hairstyle gave him a slightly gangsterish appearance, as if he had switched careers and was now John Gotti's accountant.

"Shit," said Anne under her breath. "It's my slimy next door neighbor," she added when Jason looked at her quizzically. "There's an empty table over by the bar," she said, nodding at it with her chin. "Why don't we sit there?"

"Too late," said Jason with a sigh. "He's coming over."

"Anne. How nice to see you. Enjoying the exhibit?" The doctor leaned in and Anne realized a second too late that he was going to kiss her. Her head jerked back as his lips brushed her cheek and the plate she was holding tilted precariously. An asparagus stalk rolled off and plopped onto the doctor's gray suede loafers. His mouth tightened in annoyance as he surveyed the damage. A snail trail of shiny asparagus juice meandered across his instep.

"Why don't I carry this for you," he said as he confiscated her plate and headed back to his table with it.

Anne glared at his retreating back, but followed. She had no choice. He had her mini-quiches.

As Anne approached the doctor's table she realized that he had a dining companion. A tall, straight-backed woman with bouffant white hair and hard gray eyes was sipping champagne, a disapproving expression on her bony face. Anne wondered if it was the champagne or the company which was sub-standard.

"Lady Soames, may I present my neighbor, Anne Lambert."

Anne politely extended her hand. The elderly woman looked at it as if she was checking for dirt under Anne's fingernails. Anne was about to pull her hand back when Lady Soames suddenly seized it and gave it a brief, grudging shake. Anne sat down, surreptitiously sliding her chair away from the doctor's, who had set her plate down next to his. Jason pulled out the chair on her left.

"This is Jason Gilbert," she said as she speared an asparagus. "Jason, this is Dr. John Davidson, my neighbor."

The nod they gave each other was not much friendlier than Lady Soames' handshake. Anne tried her baby roast potatoes. They had a crunchy, rosemary-flavored crust which was just heavenly.

"Anne, you don't have any champagne," said Jason. "Of course. You couldn't carry it, could you." He nodded at the cast on her left arm. "Let me get you some. Can I get anyone else anything?"

"I'd like another glass of wine," Lady Soames announced imperiously. "The Sauvignon Blanc."

Jason nodded and headed off toward the bar.

The doctor turned to Anne. "So, are you a Joseph Beuys fan?."

"No, I'm afraid I'd never heard of him. A friend of mine gave me the ticket." One of Lindsey's suitors had offered Lindsey the ticket as an expensive example of his devotion. Apparently the offering (or the offerer) had been deemed inadequate, for Lindsey had passed it on to Anne. The object of tonight's gala was to raise money for one of Princess Anne's favorite charities – Hugs For Horses – and even the cheapest tickets went for two-hundred pounds. The thousand-pounders got you a two-second handshake with the Princess and a table within spitting distance of her minders.

"I have to admit, I don't care much for the artwork, but the food is great."

"It's tolerable," said Lady Soames with a sniff, finishing off the last sip of wine in her glass. Her mouth puckered as if she'd just drunk undiluted lemon juice.

Anne dropped her gaze in embarrassment. She brushed a smattering of quiche crumbs off her lap and wondered how soon she could leave without being rude.

"I'm so sorry for your loss," Anne said, just to break the silence. She aimed a sympathetic smile at Lady Soames, who stared at her blankly.

"The loss of your son," said Anne. "Jimmy."

"Yes, it was a terrible tragedy for the entire Soames family," said Dr. Davidson when Lady Soames remained silent. The doctor leaned back, draping an arm over the back of Anne's chair. Anne's back muscles stiffened so much that her ramrod-straight posture now mirrored that of Lady Soames.

"Have you known the Soames family long?" asked Anne. It was more than just idle conversation. She was genuinely curious. The doctor seemed to be presenting himself as the family spokesman.

"Nearly twenty years now. I first met Lady Soames when she came to visit her sons at their school in Kent." He turned to Lady Soames and gave her a gallant smile. The severe expression on Lady

Soames' bony face relaxed into a graceful acceptance of the flattery.

Anne felt her stomach turn. The two of them seemed to have some sort of weird parasitical relationship, though it was difficult to tell who was the host and who the parasite. "That would be Wyndham Preparatory, the school mentioned in that anonymous note I showed you?"

The doctor's pale, hairless hand contracted suddenly around his champagne glass. His grip on it was so tight Anne wondered if the glass was going to shatter. A long, silent minute passed. Lady Soames retreated back into her severe shell. Anne kept a wary eye on the doctor, as traces of anger flickered across his immobile face like cracks in the flat crust of the desert after an earthquake.

"Yes," Dr. Davidson finally replied, his voice tense but controlled. "I began my career there, as the school's guidance counselor. Jimmy and Daniel Soames both got sent to my office several times. Just the usual boyhood indiscretions."

"Then why . . ." began Anne, but the doctor covered her hand with his and gave it a condescending pat.

"Now," he said, "Let's not upset Lady Soames with talk of Jimmy's past. We're here to forget our troubles and enjoy ourselves."

"But . . ." Anne tried again, her voice suddenly failing when the doctor squeezed her hand, crushing her fingers together.

"Here you go." Jason was back. He set Lady Soames' wine down and gave her a winsome smile, which she ignored. Undeterred, he resumed his seat next to Anne. "They were out of champagne, so I got you a coke instead. I hope that's okay." He offered a frosted tumbler full of coke and ice to Anne.

She wrested her hand free from the doctor's grasp and took the glass. "That's fine. I prefer soft drinks anyway. Never been big on alcohol." She wrapped her throbbing hand around the cold glass. She stared at her hand, silently calling the doctor every profane thing she could think of.

Jason was tucking enthusiastically into his food. "Eat up girl," he said as melted Edam dripped down his chin. "These little quiche thingys are great."

It was, of course, an accident. Anne's elbow was completely blameless. The doctor's champagne glass was just asking for trouble, sitting there so close to the edge of the table. Dr. Davidson leapt up, cursing as the damp stain spread across the crotch of his pale gray trousers.

ANNE HOOKED HER Sainsburys bag over her cast, arm sagging from the weight of her weekly grocery shop, and opened the mailbox with her other hand. A bill from London Electricity, a garish purple flyer from a new Balti restaurant, and a square-shaped envelope made of heavy paper the color of buttermilk. Odd. Kind of fancy for junk mail. She checked the return address. Lady Belinda Soames. Yikes! Daniel's mother. And Jimmy's.

She flexed her sore fingers as unpleasant memories of last night's gala at the Tate came back to her – Lady Soames' rudeness, Dr. Davidson's boorishness, Jason's . . . okay, not all of the memories were unpleasant. Jason had sent her a text message, which arrived the next day while she was at work. She'd had to ask Nick to decipher it for her. Nothing like hip, twenty-something hieroglyphics to make a person feel ready for the old-folks home. The gist of the message was a desire to see her again. Anne hadn't replied yet. Jason seemed like a nice guy, but his age was a bit of a turn off. She wanted to feel like his date, not his babysitter. She decided to do a Scarlett O'Hara and think about it tomorrow.

She slid the grocery bag off her arm and dumped it on the floor of the lobby. Opening the envelope from Lady Soames with one hand was a bit of a struggle, but she finally managed it once she got her teeth involved.

Inside was a cream colored card. A falcon stretched its wings in the red and black family crest at the top. The handwriting was an elegant cursive.

'Dear Miss Lambert,' it began, 'I enjoyed meeting you at the Tate exhibit. I and my husband feel great regret at your accident. My son Daniel mentioned that his car was involved, apparently stolen by thieves. We all wish you a speedy recovery from your injuries. We are having a small house party the weekend of March 9th, and would be delighted if you could join us. Dress is casual. I look forward to seeing you. Sincerely, Lady Belinda Soames.'

A thin sheet of paper with map and directions was clipped to the back of the card.

Huh. Anne stared at it perplexedly. Why on earth would Lady Soames be inviting her to a house party? She absently tapped the card against her chin. The Soames family must be worried about the accident. And the fact that Daniel's car was involved. Maybe his parents thought she was going to sue them. They were going to wine and dine her at this party in the hope that it would prevent her American litigious instinct from kicking in. It had never occurred to her to sue, and she wasn't going to now.

Something was off about the invitation. Lady Soames had barely acknowledged her last night at the Tate exhibit. Anne frowned at the card in her hand. She wondered if this invitation was the doctor's idea. She awkwardly tried to tuck the card back into its envelope with her teeth.

"Let me help you with that." A large, faultlessly manicured hand reached over her shoulder and plucked the invitation out of her grasp.

"I hope you'll attend," said Dr. Davidson as he read the card. "You'll enjoy it. The Soames family estate is quite impressive. It might be a bit wet this time of year, but the rhododendrons will be in bloom." He tucked the card into the envelope and handed it to her. "I'm driving down early Saturday morning. I could give you a lift."

He waited, a mocking look on his face. He had thrown down the gauntlet.

Anne refused to pick it up. She turned her back on him and stalked off toward the stairs, her attempt at affronted dignity somewhat hampered by the grocery bag banging against her legs.

Chapter Six

T HE 9:15 FROM Paddington pulled out right on time. Anne stared blankly out the window, her overnight bag tucked beneath her feet. Ominous thoughts about the weekend ahead kept making incursions into her mind. She had decided to accept Lady Soames' invitation. The chance to get an up-close-and-personal look at a big English estate had proven irresistible, but now that the moment had come she was having second thoughts.

She was nervous about meeting Lord Soames, not looking forward to seeing Lady Soames again, and definitely not thrilled at the idea of seeing Daniel again, but they were just foot-soldiers in the army of her inner demons. Dr. Davidson was the Panzer tank brigade. She wondered if he was going to be orchestrating the whole weekend. Directing the Soames family like a courtroom defense lawyer. She couldn't help feeling that they were marshalling a defense against her. The irony was that she had no intention of attacking them. She felt sorry for Jimmy Soames and his early demise, but it was the job of the police to track down his killer, if in fact he'd even been murdered. She wasn't about to stick her nose into the tragedy. Surely his parents realized that.

At Fairhill Station, the stop closest to the Soames estate, Anne was the only passenger to alight from the train. She passed through the deserted red brick station and paused uncertainly outside its front entrance. Fairhill was definitely not a major transportation hub. Lady

Soames' directions stated that taxis could be found at the station, but there were none in evidence. A ticket office – closed – and a vending machine offering Cadbury's Fruit and Nut bars were the only amenities. She set her bag down on a weather-beaten bench and pulled out the sheet of directions. The Soames estate was two miles from the station. Not a difficult walk for someone used to jogging three miles every day. Plus her overnight bag was light. Anne checked the map Lady Soames had drawn and set out.

THIRTY MINUTES LATER she reached the gates of the Soames estate. The walk had been pleasant enough. It was a gray day, but not rainy, and car traffic was light. For the last half-mile a wall of roughly hewn stone blocks had bordered the road. The wall ended in two stone turrets flanking a wrought-iron gate. Pale green moss covered the crumbling turrets, and the left-hand one had a falcon carved into it – the Soames family crest which she'd noticed on her invitation. The gates were closed, but a pedestrian-sized door in the wall was ajar. She passed through.

Trees bordered the gravel drive in front of her on both sides, ancient oaks and the occasional pine, with purple banks of rhododendrons looking phosphorescent in the gloom. The only noise came from drops of water falling from the leaves and rustlings where the squirrels were going about their business in the branches. The drive wound around for a hundred yards or so, then the trees thinned out and Anne emerged into open parkland. Shallow, grass-covered mounds, like snowboarding moguls, stretched in every direction. The effect was golf course minus the golfers. The house was straight ahead, its turrets reflected in a reed-bordered lake. Anne tried to guess the age of the building, maybe 18th century with a few older pieces here and there. Like many big estates, it had been added onto by each successive owner until the final result resembled a jigsaw puzzle with several pieces missing. It was imposing rather than pretty, which probably suited the family just fine. The facade was gray stone, with two large stone lions guarding the front steps. They had assumed the Sphinx position – muscular haunches lowered, front paws out-stretched, regal faces fixed on some mystery only they could see. If they were protecting the house from the non-aristocratic then they should be roaring loudly by now, Anne thought as she climbed the stairs.

She hesitated in front of a massive medieval oaken door. The carved figure of a falcon, its wings outstretched, hovered over a group of faceless men in bishops miters. A pair of muddy wellies stood next to the mat. No doorbell was in evidence, but a length of braided velvet rope hung beside the door. She gave it a tentative pull and heard a muted bell peal somewhere inside the house. A short silence, and then footsteps clacked across a marble floor. Anne stepped back from the door as it opened.

"Good morning Ma'am. You must be Miss Lambert. Please come in." A pleasant looking, gray-haired man swung the door open wider. "Lady Soames is in the Morning Room. If you'll just follow me." He turned down a hallway lined with portraits, probably the family ancestors, Anne guessed. Before trotting after him she let her gaze roam across the entrance hall of the building. An expanse of white marble led to twin staircases which curved to meet each other at a landing facing the front door. An ornately framed mirror on the landing reflected the pink clouds and blue sky of a painting opposite. It depicted a Greek god flying across the heavens in a chariot. Probably an early Soames ancestor, thought Anne wryly.

She hurried to catch up with the gray-haired gentleman. He slipped noiselessly into a walnut-paneled room which branched off main the hallway, approaching a woman who was writing at a desk by the window. He waited patiently for her to finish, and when she set her pen down announced – "Miss Lambert."

Anne scurried forward, hand extended. Lady Soames rose in one graceful motion and briefly clasped Anne's hand, her expression plainly showing that she wished she had on the gloves she normally donned before meeting Americans. Anne surreptitiously checked her fingernails for dirt. Nope. Clean. Even the ones protruding from her cast.

"Carstairs, bring us some tea please," ordered Lady Soames as she glided across the room and settled onto a sofa covered in pale blue satin. Anne gingerly perched at the other end. She rubbed a finger along the smooth fabric. It reminded her of the chair covered in silk in Dr. Davidson's office. Didn't these people ever spill anything?

She studied Lady Soames warily. Her hostess seemed less irritable than she had at their last meeting at the Tate Modern. Her demeanor had shifted from rude to politely distant. She wore an elegant cream-colored jersey dress, with a boxy blue linen jacket on top. The jacket looked like a ten-pound special from TopShop. Anne wondered if this was one of those quirky upper-class affectations.

"I understand you've met my son Daniel," said Lady Soames.

"Um, yes," replied Anne. "He came to see me at my office."

"I suggested that he do so. We wanted you to know that the family was grieved by your accident, even though we were not of course involved."

Since one of the family's cars had been used to turn her into road-kill Anne wasn't quite sure how to respond to this. She also decided it would be best not to mention that Daniel had tried to forcibly drag her out of her office. Possibly the rich considered that kind of thing just a social custom, like air-kissing.

"I believe you also knew my son James."

Anne looked at her blankly for a minute before the piece clicked into place. "Oh, right. Jimmy. Again, I'm very sorry for your loss," she added.

Lady Soames nodded briefly.

Anne paused. Carstairs had come in bearing a Royal Doulton tea service. He poured out two cups and set a tray with lemon slices, sugar cubes, milk, and a plate of delicate pink-frosted cakes down onto the coffee table next to the sofa. Anne carefully picked up the teacup closest to her. It was bone china covered with sprays of red roses and gilded around the rim. Pretty in an over the top sort of way.

"I didn't actually know Jimmy. We'd only met briefly, at Dr. Davidson's flat."

"Yes. John Davidson told me. Dear man. We've been friends for years. He was such a help to James during his difficult periods. The doctor was the school counselor at Wyndham Preparatory here in Kent. James had great difficulty fitting in with the other boys, and John helped him through that. I don't know what we would have done without him." She added two sugar cubes and a squeeze of lemon to her tea. "James was always a bit of a dreamer," she continued with a disapproving expression. "My husband tried many times to interest him in the family business, with no success. James just had no head for business. Daniel is much more practical. He has no compunction about going after what he wants."

Something about the way Lady Soames said this caused Anne to look up at her sharply. The older woman's expression was unreadable, her gaze focused on the tea she was stirring with a tiny silver spoon, but her last statement had triggered an unexpected idea in Anne's mind. She had the distinct, and shocking, impression that Lady Soames suspected Daniel of killing his brother – and that she wasn't all that upset by the thought.

ANNE SPLASHED COLD water on her face and tried to convince herself she was ready for the trials to come. Carstairs had knocked on the door of her room and imparted the news that lunch was ready in the Ludden dining room. She turned off the taps and checked in the mirror to make sure she was presentable enough to eat in a room which had its own name. Very spiffy, she told herself encouragingly. She had on her best t-shirt, a black one from The Gap, bought only two weeks ago. No noticeable stains or holes on either her shirt or her jeans. Okay, so there was that ink stain on her left knee, but you'd have to be crawling around on your hands and knees to notice it.

She gave her hair a quick brush and plopped down on the pink satin bedspread to tie a loose shoelace, carefully holding the muddy sole away from the fabric. The bedroom Lady Soames had assigned her was small but elegant, with a heavy oak four-poster bed, matching bureau, and brass floor lamps with rose satin shades echoing the bedspread. A marble fireplace with cherubs gamboling across the mantle faced the bed, and a window seat with a tapestry cushion looked out over the lake. The room was comfortable and cozy, but its elegance left Anne feeling twitchy. She was afraid to touch anything for fear of staining or breaking it. Upper class life took some getting used to. She would have felt more at ease in a cheap Bed & Breakfast. She nervously tucked in her t-shirt for the third time, then left the room and hurried along the wood-paneled hall to the stairs leading down to the first floor. These stairs were a work of art. Entirely made of white marble, the banister was covered with marble roses and ripe grape vines twisting in all directions. Anne traced a stone rose petal with a fingertip as she passed, its coldness sending a chill up her arm.

She reached the bottom of the stairs and paused to scout around for landmarks. A vase full of yellow tulips stood on a small malachite table to her left. She didn't remember passing it when Carstairs had shown her up to her room. She glanced to the right. A long hallway carpeted in pale gold seemed familiar. Anne started down this, peeking in each room that branched off of it. She remembered a dark, oak-paneled room with a pool table. Here it was. Now, through here and then across this foyer, then . . . Aargh! She was lost. Three hallways branched off the foyer like entrances to a labyrinth. Did she take the left-hand one, only to be devoured by a snarling tiger? Or the middle one, to be crushed by falling boulders? Or the right-hand one, where a pirate's hoard of gold and jewels sparkled? Even dismemberment by tiger seemed preferable to the lunch party which awaited. Maybe if she wandered around the house long enough lunch would be over before she got there.

"It's the right-hand one," said a voice behind her.

Anne whirled around. It was Dr. Davidson. He was more casually dressed than usual, in a gray cashmere pullover and darker gray trousers. The pleats on his trousers were ironed to a knife-edge sharpness.

"You startled me," gasped Anne, stating the obvious.

Dr. Davidson smiled his barely-there smile and didn't apologize.

Anne was tempted to ask where he had come from, but decided she didn't want to know. She preferred to think that his guest room was at the opposite end of the house from hers. If the reality was more unpleasant than that, well, she'd rather be uninformed. There were times when self-delusion was the key to sanity.

"I hope your room is satisfactory." He motioned toward the correct hallway and politely waited for her. The corridor had large floor-to-ceiling windows looking out toward the back of the house. As they walked Anne caught glimpses of a French-style formal garden. Low box hedges were trimmed into intricate knot patterns and bordered by gravel walks. The turned-over earth of dormant flowerbeds looked like rich chocolate cake trampled on by the gardener.

"My room is fine, thanks."

"I have the corner room two doors down from you," the doctor said, seeming to read her thoughts. "Lady Soames always puts me there when I visit." His tone implied that he was a frequent guest at the Soames estate, and was well aware of the status this imparted. "The family bedrooms are in another wing, so our rooms are quite isolated. I find it very restful."

Anne didn't respond. She was preoccupied in trying to recall if her room had a lock on the door. She didn't think so.

After a few more twists and turns they finally emerged into the Ludden dining room. Anne had no idea how to find her way back to her room. A trail of breadcrumbs might have been wise, she thought to herself.

The room was smaller than she had expected, with an ordinary-sized dining table in its center. Blue brocade fabric covered the walls and chair backs. French doors opened onto a section of the terrace which had been enclosed in glass – a decorative greenhouse where orange and grapefruit trees looked out of place against the cold rain pelting the glass.

Lady Soames was already seated at one end of the dining table, her posture rigid and uninviting. A tall, broad-shouldered man with wavy gray hair faced her over a centerpiece stuffed with white mums and spiky dahlias. Lord Soames, Anne guessed. Daniel was pacing back and forth, chewing on his thumbnail. He stopped when she entered and gave her a furtive look before slumping into his chair. Dr. Davidson pulled out a chair for her and waited beside it. Anne eyed him suspiciously. She was tempted to ignore him and take the other empty chair, but was afraid of looking childish. She gingerly sat down on the edge of the chair, leaning away from him as he pushed her up to the table.

"Jack, this is Miss Lambert," said Lady Soames by way of introduction.

Anne aimed a hesitant smile toward the end of the table. Lord Soames nodded at her curtly and then opened the Financial Times with a snap. Anne dropped her eyes to her plate in embarrassment and then glanced up to find Daniel staring at her fixedly. He was still chewing on his thumbnail, which was beginning to resemble a bloody piece of steak tartare.

"Got my car back," he said. "The police returned it yesterday, no thanks to you."

"Daniel!" barked Lady Soames.

Daniel slumped further into his chair and wrapped a white linen handkerchief around his thumb, watching with interest as a spot of blood soaked through it.

He was better than any diet pill ever made, thought Anne as she watched him. She now had no appetite whatsoever, which was inconvenient, as Carstairs was hovering at her elbow with a tray of sliced beef in horseradish sauce. Anne took a small piece and pushed it to the edge of her plate. She took a sip of water and wondered not for the first time what she was doing there. It was Saturday, and the earliest she could politely leave was probably Sunday, around noon. A whole twenty-four hours to go. She permitted herself an inaudible sigh. The house was beautiful, but the attractions of the estate were considerably diminished by the personalities of its owners.

"Daniel is a trader, you know," exclaimed Lady Soames suddenly. "In the City. He's quite the expert on stocks and bonds."

Lord Soames grunted at this in a way which didn't suggest proud papa. Dr. Davidson hid a smile behind his napkin.

"Everyone at his company is quite impressed with him," continued Lady Soames. "The chairman mentioned it only last week. You remember, Jack. At the club."

"I suspect what he was impressed with was the golf course," replied Lord Soames dryly.

Lady Soames chose to ignore this. She helped herself to a piece of bread and passed the basket to Anne. "We were thinking of taking a little trip this afternoon to Daniel's old school, Wyndham Preparatory, if the weather clears. It's not far from here, and the campus is beautiful. I always enjoy taking a walk around it. Plus I want to check on James' memorial. We authorized the construction of a new gymnasium in his honor. He always enjoyed sport."

Daniel began coughing loudly at this, but Lady Soames' selective hearing screened him out. "Would you care to come with us?" she asked Anne.

"Um, yes. Sure. That would be nice," Anne replied, wondering who exactly was included in the 'us'.

AN HOUR LATER Anne found herself in the cushy back seat of a silver Bentley, squashed between Lady Soames and Dr. Davidson. She had her North Face parka wrapped around her, her arms folded, and her legs tightly crossed at the ankles. In short, she was making herself as small as humanly possible, and yet Dr. Davidson's knee still kept mysteriously bumping hers. Each time it did she twitched away as if she'd been shocked with a bare electric wire.

Carstairs was driving and Daniel was in the front seat next to him, smoking furiously. The car's windows were closed against the cold March weather and the front seat was beginning to resemble Los Angeles on a smog-alert day. Anne was grateful for the clear glass barrier which separated the front seat from the back. Now, if she could just open the back door and give Dr. Davidson a shove – preferably when they were doing over sixty – then the drive might actually be enjoyable. The Kent countryside they were passing through was pretty in a low-key sort of way. Rolling hills, clumps of woodland, fields of hops newly planted and ready for spring. The road was bordered on both sides by untrimmed hedgerows which partially blocked the view. Anne didn't notice the sign for the school until they had passed it. Out of the corner of her eye she caught the word 'Preparatory' in gold letters on a blue background just as they turned off the main road. She hadn't noticed a town or even a farm for more than a mile. The school seemed to be unusually isolated.

They drove past a swampy looking football pitch with dozens of little boys sliding around in the mud, their green and white jerseys rapidly turning brown. A lot of students around for a Saturday, thought Anne. Then she remembered that this was a boarding school. The students were stuck here all year round. She felt a twinge of pity for them, especially the older ones. It must drive the teenagers crazy to live in the middle of nowhere, with no town center to hang out in.

The football pitches and dormitories they passed were modern and characterless, but as they approached the center of the campus the buildings went back in time. Several were Georgian in style, all straight lines and yellow brick. Farther in a stately group of Tudor mansions huddled together, their sides almost touching. At the very center an elegant sweep of green lawn stretched between ancient oak trees.

Carstairs parked the Bentley next to a crumbling stone church. While Dr. Davidson helped Lady Soames on with her coat Anne wandered over to the church. A wooden sign planted in the grass next to its roman-arched entrance was plastered with notices printed on pink paper. Choir practice was Saturdays at noon, she read. The vicar's cat (black with a white spot on its nose) had gone missing, as had ten of the church's altar candles. Listed below the notices were the times the church was open for business. Sunday services were at 9:00 a.m., and something called Evensong happened on Wednesdays. Anne wondered what this was. She climbed the flagstone steps at the front of the church and tried the battered black door. Locked.

She turned to go back down the stairs – and nearly ploughed into Dr. Davidson. He grabbed her by the shoulders to keep her from falling into him. She shuddered at the contact and jerked away.

"What?" Anne snapped.

"Nothing," replied the doctor, raising his hands in a 'calm down, I wasn't doing anything' gesture. "I was just wondering if you'd like to see the building where I used to work. It has a stunning Adams ceiling in the front hall, and even a small Gainsborough in the headmaster's office."

"Um, sure, I guess," Anne said. "Who else is coming?"

"Daniel," replied the doctor with a slight smile. "Lady Soames and Carstairs are walking over to the gymnasium. We'll meet up with

68

them later. It's this way." He gestured toward a clump of leafless oaks. Daniel fell in behind them, muttering to himself in between drags on his cigarette.

As they drew nearer a building became visible through the trees. A two-story brick mansion in the Tudor style, its walls mottled by age and lichen, its chimneys leaning toward each other like office workers gossiping about the boss. Dr. Davidson led the way up the front steps, his feet following the grooves worn into the stone by generations.

The doctor paused inside the entrance hall and pointed up at the ceiling. "Adams. About 1770."

Anne looked up. A complex pattern of stucco grape vines spiraled around the edge of the ceiling and snaked down the columns positioned at each of the room's corners. "It's beautiful," she said. And meant it.

Daniel was less impressed with the room's attractions. He leaned against the nearest column and lit another cigarette.

"You can't smoke in here," snapped the doctor. "This is a listed building. Do you realize what damage smoke can do to plasterwork?"

Daniel stared at him blankly, the cigarette hanging from his lip. Finally, he pulled it from his mouth and dropped it on the marble floor of the hall. He sauntered out the front door like a rebellious schoolboy overly impressed with a small act of defiance.

Dr. Davidson grimaced in disgust and carefully squashed the butt with his shoe, then picked it up and wiped the floor with his handkerchief.

"Who's been smoking in here?" a voice suddenly roared from the corridor leading off the entrance hall. Footsteps echoed around the hall and then stopped as a portly, bearded man in a black suit and gray-striped vest appeared. "Davidson!" he shouted in surprise. "What are you doing here and why are you smoking while doing it?"

"I'm just visiting," the doctor replied calmly. "And the smoke belongs to a former pupil, Daniel Soames."

"Soames," grunted the bearded gentleman. "I remember him. Wish I didn't. Weasely little git. Won't amount to anything, despite his family's money."

"Very true," agreed a nondescript looking man in a brown tweed suit who had followed his loud colleague into the hall. "I had him in one of my European History classes. He sat in the back row all term. I suspect he was asleep most of the time."

"I'm sure he wasn't the only one," said the doctor mildly.

The bearded gentleman chuckled at this and gave his colleague a slap on the back which rocked him like a rowboat in a storm. "Yes, Kenneth's style of teaching lacks drama. That's what the boys want. You can't stand up there whispering at them. Davidson," he continued, "Why don't you join us in my office? I have a bottle of Madeira which needs sampling. Your friend is welcome too of course," he said with a polite nod at Anne.

Anne returned his nod, but recognized a chance for escape when she saw it. "Thank you, that's very tempting, but I'd like to have a walk around your campus. You have some beautiful buildings here."

"Yes, we do," said the man in the brown suit. "Why don't we leave them to their port. I'll show you around a bit. I'm by way of an architecture buff. Goes hand in hand with the teaching of history. What do you say?"

Anne was a little taken aback at this offer, but recovered quickly. Anything to remove herself from Dr. Davidson's company. "Sure. That would be nice."

"AND THIS IS our Philosophy and Psychology building. Queen Anne style, built about 1850."

Anne and Kenneth, as he had insisted she call him, were standing on a flagstone path which had lost a battle with tree roots. The path buckled and writhed in agony where oak roots as fat as pythons snaked under it. The knarled oaks themselves looked as if they were trying their best to ignore the violence at their feet.

"Psychology," said Anne. "Then this is the building where Dr. Davidson worked."

"No," replied the history professor apologetically. "The Administration building – the one with the Adams ceiling – that's where he worked. He didn't teach Psychology. He was the school's guidance counselor. I'm sure he's glad to be away from it and in private practice. Between you and me, he was not very good at interacting with the boys. The only boy who seemed to be comfortable in his presence was James Soames. You know, Daniel's brother."

"Yes. I met him once, about a month ago," said Anne. "Only a week before his death."

"Yes. Very sad," said Kenneth, picking at a loose thread on his jacket sleeve. "I've read the accounts of it in the papers. Not that they've given it much coverage. James didn't make any more impression in death than he did in life. But regardless, the papers have hinted at foul play."

"Yes," said Anne. "Do you think anyone might have had a grudge against him?" she asked.

"I have no idea," said the professor. "James graduated more than a decade ago, and I haven't seen him since. Of course, we see Lord and Lady Soames here occasionally. They are great benefactors of the school. And Daniel comes to alumni events. Actually, I could easily see someone doing away with Daniel. He tends to antagonize people. James, on the other hand, has always sort of faded into the background. Never involved in any kind of controversy. Well, except for the incident of that young boy's strangulation."

Anne's eyebrows went up into her hairline. "What young boy?" she managed to squeak out.

"Oh, this was years ago. James was still a student here, though he was close to graduating if I remember correctly. A ten year old boy was found strangled in the dorms. There was, of course, an exacting investigation. It went on for more than a year, with the police here constantly. All of the staff and students were questioned, but there was little physical evidence. In the end the police had to concede defeat. As far as I know the case is still open. Anyway, the reason the incident rose to my mind is that James Soames was under suspicion for a while. The police interrogated him at great length, but no actual charges were ever brought. I don't remember why the police focused on him. Davidson would probably know. He spent a great deal of time counseling James during that year. James would have been only fifteen, maybe sixteen, with his whole life ahead of him. The prospect of a lengthy jail sentence would shake stronger souls than his."

Blackmail. The word leapt into Anne's mind the second the teacher finished. As they turned and started the walk back to the Administration building she stretched and pulled the idea to see if it fit the facts. Yes, it made perfect sense. Dr. Davidson found out that Jimmy Soames had killed this ten year old boy. Possibly Jimmy had admitted it during a counseling session. The Soames family was very wealthy. Jimmy would have made an ideal candidate for blackmail. The doctor must have been furious when Jimmy was murdered. Someone had cut off his money supply.

"It couldn't have been *that* fascinating."

"What?" Anne looked up, startled to find herself back at the Administration building and face to face with Dr. Davidson.

"The tour of the campus. I suspect Kenneth the tour guide is just as soporific as Kenneth the lecturer."

"Possibly," said the professor acidly, "but I believe Miss Lambert was entertained by my last topic. I was telling her about that police investigation we had years ago. That young boy who was strangled. You remember, Davidson. You were here at the time."

"Yes, I was," said the doctor, looking thoughtfully at Anne.

Anne could feel herself begin to sweat with the effort to maintain a neutral expression. It wasn't until the doctor turned away to greet an approaching Lady Soames that she realized she was holding her breath. She exhaled sharply and followed Lady Soames and the doctor as they walked back to the Bentley.

Carstairs was standing by the car waiting for them.

"Have you seen Daniel?" Lady Soames barked at him.

"No ma'am, I haven't. I'll go search for him if you like."

"Do that," snapped Lady Soames. "The Bishop and his wife are coming over for tea in less than an hour. If we keep them waiting I'll never hear the end of it. That woman will make sure the entire county knows. I've never met anyone so fond of gossiping about her betters."

THEY MADE IT back in time for tea. The Bishop and his wife arrived just as Carstairs entered the Music Room bearing chicken salad sandwiches on an enormous silver tray. He set this down with a flourish onto a damask-covered table in the middle of the room. Seven chairs with matching petit-point embroidered seats were grouped loosely around the table. Anne selected one at the outer edge of the group and awaited developments. She wasn't sure of the protocol here – did you just grab a sandwich, or wait to be served? Better to wait and copy the actions of someone else – though not Daniel, who had thrown himself onto a tufted leather couch at the far end of the room and immediately begun to snore. Everyone else politely took their seats and waited for Lady Soames to take the lead. She signaled to Carstairs, who distributed cups of Earl Grey and plates stacked with sandwiches, cream-filled scones, and bite-size chocolate gateau which reminded Anne of Ding-Dongs.

Anne munched quietly and watched as the new arrivals made their obeisance to Lady Soames. The Bishop was a large, vague man dressed in a conventional business suit. He apparently felt he'd done his share by kissing the hand of his hostess. After this feat he sat crumbling a scone and staring fixedly at the carpet. His wife, wrapped in a striking silver fox coat which she refused to remove, felt it her duty to make up the verbal slack created by her husband. She talked incessantly throughout the meal, patting her blonde beehive and taking tiny nibbles of her sandwich without stopping for breath. Their house near Leeds Castle was her main topic. Each time she mentioned this paragon of the decorator's arts its nearness to the Castle increased. By the end of the meal she and the Bishop were on the cusp of installing themselves in the Castle's Keep, tour groups be damned. After all, it was good enough for Lady Baillie.

AFTER SURVIVING TEA with the Bishop's wife Anne felt in need of some solitude. She excused herself to take a walk around the grounds. Lady Soames seemed grateful to be relieved of the burden of entertaining her, Daniel was still snoring in the Music Room, and Lord Soames was nowhere to be found. The only threat to her plan was Dr. Davidson, who looked ready to accompany her until Lady Soames beckoned to him with a bony hand. When Anne was sure that he was safely in the clutches of Lady Soames and the Bishop's wife she made good her escape. She donned her parka, which Carstairs produced as if by magic, zipped it up against the cold March afternoon, and slipped out the front door. She patted one of the stone lions on the head and halted at the bottom of the steps. The gravel at her feet was mottled with small puddles. She titled her head back and looked up at the sky. It was only 4:00 p.m., but clouds heavy with unshed rain had bullied the sun into hiding. It was gloomy walking weather, but anything was better than listening to the Bishop's wife expound on Kent property values.

Anne turned to her left towards the lake. She strolled along a strip of lawn speckled with dandelions, her shoes making squelching noises in the wet grass. The house's many windows stared down at her as if warning her not to return, but soon the house was left behind as the grass gave way to a gravel path. Anne continued along this as it followed the curve of the lake. She wound through a thicket of aspens, their leaves rustling in the damp breeze. Tiny bluebells waved in the uncut grass under the trees. The path ran over a small hill, and then halted at the edge of the water, where a wooden pier jutted out into the lake.

Anne walked out to the end of the pier, its planks creaking with each step. It was peaceful out over the water. She perched on a tar-stained post and listened to the silence. The estate was so far back from the road that traffic noises didn't penetrate. She couldn't see the house anymore. A small spit of land covered with aspen and fir blocked her view. No clipped lawn bordered the lake here. The landscape had been left wild and trees came down to the edge of the water.

A tiny quack broke the silence. Anne leaned forward, but didn't see any ducks on the lake. She pushed herself off the post and knelt at the edge of the pier. Leaning on her elbows she craned her neck until she could see underneath. There. A mallard and her three babies were clustered together against the post Anne had been sitting on. The mother began quacking loudly, startled by Anne's shadow floating toward them over the water.

"Sshhh. It's okay," said Anne to the duck. The duck refused to be soothed, and herded her brood farther under the pier. Anne stretched forward but soon lost sight of them, the last duckling paddling furiously after its mother like a tiny wind-up toy.

Anne started to straighten up, her arms feeling the strain of leaning at such a sharp angle, when suddenly she felt a violent shove on her back. She lost her balance and fell face first into the water.

The lake was freezing cold and dense with algae. The muddy bottom sucked at Anne's feet. She surfaced, gasping and spitting water. Her first instinct was to swim, but her thrashing feet hit the bottom of the lake and she realized that it was shallow enough to stand. She stopped kicking and straightened her legs. The water came up to her chin. She coughed again and shoved a clump of wet hair out of her eyes. What a nasty practical joke, she thought as she headed for the pier. Daniel. It seemed like something he would do. Maybe his twisted little mind considered this payback for refusing to help him get his precious Mercedes back from the police.

Anne put a hand on the edge of the pier and looked up. She couldn't see anyone, but the boards were creaking. Someone was there. She glanced down, looking for a foothold on the post. Suddenly she felt something on the top of her head. It was a hand, pushing her down. It was so unexpected that she lost her grip on the post and slid under the water. The hand followed. She reached up, trying to dislodge it, but it was too strong. She was panicking, swallowing dirty lake water, but she had just enough rational thought left to try moving sideways, away from the hand. She felt the pressure on her head lessen and pushed desperately against the lake bottom, trying to get her head above water. She managed it for just an instant, gasping and choking, before she felt the hand grip her by the shoulder and push her under again. This time she couldn't free herself from its grip. The water churned from her struggles, and then grew still.

Chapter Seven

I T WAS DARK. Open your eyes you idiot, thought Anne. Better. Not dark yet, but getting there. It must be about 5:00 p.m. The short March afternoon was rapidly fading to evening. She yawned. It was a strange time for a nap. And a strange place. She was not in her own bed. This one was much more posh, with a pale pink satin quilt and tall bedposts at each corner. She glanced around foggily, the brown leather of her overnight bag catching her eye. Oh, right. She was in Lady Soames' bed. Er, Lady Soames' guest bedroom. But what was she doing there at five in the afternoon? And why was her hair wet?

Movement. Over by the door. Anne struggled to sit up, her heart racing but her body moving in slow motion. A sharp pain shot through her left wrist. The cast was missing.

"It's okay Miss Lambert. I'm PC Ridley. How are you feeling?" The police constable who approached her was a blonde woman of about thirty, wearing a uniform but missing her hat, which Anne noticed on a chair by the door.

"Um, I feel okay, I guess. A bit muddled. Why am I in bed? And why are the police here?"

"I'll let the Inspector tell you that. I take it you don't remember what happened."

"Happened? What do you mean?"

The constable didn't answer. She went to the door and leaned out into the hallway. Anne saw her wave to someone. A few seconds later voices approached.

"Turner, go supervise. Make sure no one tramples the ground around the lake. We should get some good shoe prints from that mud."

Anne dragged herself to a sitting position as the voice came nearer. She noticed she was wearing an unfamiliar flannel nightgown. Someone had taken her shoes off and tucked towels and a hot-water bottle around her. Her legs and the sheets of the bed were streaked with mud and some kind of green stuff that looked like spinach. Anne shivered. She grabbed one of the towels and wrapped it around her shoulders and then pulled the pink satin bedspread up to her chin.

"Constable, take notes please," said a short man in an overcoat as he bustled into the room. Anne took this to be the Inspector. He was an average-looking gentleman of about fifty-five, with brown hair which was losing a battle with gray invaders.

"How do you do Miss Lambert. I'm Inspector Northam of the Kent Constabulary." He politely extended his hand, which Anne shook uncertainly. "As you might expect," the Inspector continued, "I need to ask you some questions about what happened."

"What exactly did happen?" asked Anne.

"Well, I was hoping you could tell us. Do you remember anything at all?"

Anne frowned and stared down at the bedspread. She was trying not to panic, but she could feel her heart racing again and her breath beginning to shorten. This was worse than the concussion she'd had after the car had hit her. She had felt disoriented then, but she'd remembered what had happened to her. This time she couldn't, and it was terrifying. A small piece of her life was missing.

The Inspector tried again. "What is the last thing you remember?"

Anne looked up at him blankly, then let her gaze roam around the room as she tried to think. "We went to the school. Wyndham Preparatory. No, wait. After that there was tea in the dining room, with the Bishop. I remember his wife and Leeds Castle. After tea I went out for a walk. I remember walking along the edge of the lake."

"What time did you leave the house?"

"About 4:00. I remember that clearly, because I was so bored at tea that I was watching the clock."

"Right. 4:00 o'clock. You left the house, started walking along the lake . . . and then what?"

"I . . . I don't know. Then I woke up here in this room."

The Inspector's shoulders slumped. Anne could tell that he was disappointed. She felt guilty, as if she'd let him down. She mentally whacked herself upside the head, trying to shake loose a few more memories, but nothing came.

"Someone tried to drown you," said the Inspector quietly.

Anne stared at him in shock, her green eyes dark in her white face. "Who . . ." she whispered.

"We don't know who. We also don't know why. Can you think of any reason why someone would want to harm you?"

"No," replied Anne.

"Can I ask you why you've come for a visit here? Are you a friend of the Soames? A relative?"

"No. Neither," replied Anne. The Inspector's eyebrows went up in surprise at this. "Lady Soames sent me an invitation to come for the weekend. I . . . I think she felt bad about the accident, and she invited me as a sort of apology." That was safe ground. The car accident was public knowledge, the police in London knew about it. No one here at the house could accuse her of making wild accusations.

"What accident?" asked the Inspector.

"I was hit by a car, in London, about two weeks ago. That's why I had a cast on my left arm. My wrist was broken."

Inspector Northam turned toward the constable. "Dr. Hopkirk removed the cast sir. It was disintegrating from the lake water."

"I see," said the Inspector, turning back to Anne. "Now, why would Lady Soames feel it necessary to apologize for this accident? Was she driving the car which hit you?"

"No," said Anne carefully. "But the car did belong to her son. To Daniel."

"Ah. Well, that makes sense then. Lady Soames was trying to apologize for her son's bad driving. Doesn't explain why anyone would try to drown you, though. I suppose it could have been a random attack, some lunatic who wandered onto the estate grounds. That would certainly be the most convenient solution," said the Inspector, doubt heavy in his voice.

"Are you sure I was attacked?" asked Anne. "I mean, maybe I just fell into the lake by accident. Hit my head on a rock or something and was knocked unconscious."

"No, it was not an accident," said the Inspector. He pointed at her left shoulder. "Take a look there."

Anne glanced at him doubtfully, then pulled the flannel night-gown off her shoulder. A deep red mark, the size of a man's hand, was shockingly dark against her skin.

"Someone held you under the water. You were found floating face down, bumping up against one of the posts of a small pier on the east side of the lake. It was Carstairs who saw you. He has a break from his duties after teatime, and it's his habit to take a daily walk around the lake. There's a path which goes all the way round and ends at the main drive. Anyway, he spotted something floating in the water when he reached the pier. He pulled you out and did his best to administer CPR. He's no doctor, of course, but he takes a course offered by the Red Cross each year. He knew enough of the basics to get you breathing again. One of our local medics, Dr. Hopkirk, lives just down the road so Carstairs called him rather than the emergency services. The doctor checked you out and pronounced you fit enough to be tucked up in bed here rather than be sent to hospital. I don't mind telling you that him and I had words about that. It was very irregular. An ambulance should have been called. I suspect one of the family had a hand in it. The Soames wield a lot of power in this county. Local people tend to do what the family tells them."

Anne frowned. "But I'm okay, aren't I? I mean, should I be concerned about brain damage and all that?"

"The doctor estimated that you'd been unconscious for less than a minute. Not enough to cause brain damage, though if I were you I'd get myself to an A & E in a hospital in London and have them check me out. Your memory loss is a bit disturbing. Haven't dealt with many drowning cases, so I don't know if it's a common side effect."

"Sir," said PC Ridley, who had been standing behind him quietly taking notes, "my last posting was on the Cornish coast. St. Ives. As you'd expect we had a lot of boating accidents and swimmers in trouble. Short term memory loss is frequently seen in near-drownings. It's caused by lack of oxygen to the brain."

The Inspector listened to her carefully. "Thank you constable. Miss Lambert does not seem to be exhibiting any other symptoms, at least to my untrained eye. What do you think?"

Anne found herself scrutinized by PC Ridley's calm blue eyes. "Disorientation and an altered mental state can occur in cases where the victim has been in the water for three minutes or more. Like yourself, I'm no medical expert, but I would say that Miss Lambert has not shown any sign of these."

"Quite. Well, this chat has been rather inconclusive," remarked the Inspector. He took a pad of yellow post-it notes out of his coat pocket, wrote something on the top sheet, and pulled it off. He handed this to Anne. "Never remember to carry business cards. These are my work and home numbers. Speaking of phone numbers, I want to give London a ring. Someone up there must have investigated your car accident. Do you have any contact details you can give me?"

"I don't know her phone number, but the name of the officer who talked to me in the hospital was Inspector Beckett. She was from the

Bishopsgate station. A constable was there also, but I can't remember his name."

"Not a problem. That's enough to be going on with. That doctor, what's his name, Davidson, gave us your address. If you could just jot down your home and office phone numbers."

Anne took the post-it pad he offered and wrote down the numbers. She was handing the pad back to him when a uniformed officer rushed into the room.

"Sir, we've got a bit of a situation downstairs. Sergeant Turner is there, but he's in over his head if you ask me. You'd better come down."

Inspector Northam studied the intruder calmly. "Hmm. Why don't you tell me more about this situation, constable, before I go blundering into it."

"Right. Yes sir. Sorry." The officer was very young, not more than twenty-two or three, and was rapidly turning pink about the ears from embarrassment. Anne noticed that he was twisting his hat in his hands, something she thought only happened in movies involving Victorian street urchins.

"You see," continued the officer, "we found a perfect set of shoe prints, both feet, in the mud just in front of the pier. We took a plaster cast, and Turner brought it into the house and quietly began comparing it to shoes in the bedrooms. He wasn't sneaky about it, exactly, but he did avoid the family members, especially Lady Soames. I think he wanted to avoid a scene."

"Very wise of him," the Inspector remarked dryly.

"Anyway," said the constable, his ears bright red by now, "it turned out that the cast was an exact match for a pair of shoes found in Daniel Soames' closet. A pair of shoes which had traces of wet mud on them." He paused and looked at Inspector Northam expectantly. If the constable was certain of a positive reaction to his news he was disappointed. The Inspector stared at him for a long moment, then took out his post-it pad and made a note on it. He tucked the pad back in his pocket.

"Hmm," he finally responded. "Damn convenient, that."

"Convenient sir?" asked the constable with a confused frown.

"Planted. Don't you ever watch American TV shows? Kojak would have spotted this as a frame up right away. Even those idiots on The Bill would have been suspicious. Of course, that doesn't mean it actually is a frame-up. Just something to keep in mind. The real criminal could have borrowed Daniel's shoes, put them on, walked out to the pier – careful to step in the mud – attacked Miss Lambert, and then returned the shoes. All speculation, of course. But plausible."

"Yes sir," said the constable doubtfully.

"I take it that the esteemed Lady Soames kicked up a ruckus when Turner tried to question Daniel."

"Exactly sir."

The Inspector sighed. "Rank has its disadvantages. Remember that you two," he said to the constables. "Well Miss Lambert, I'd better go down and deal with this. PC Ridley will be staying with you until you leave Kent. After that there isn't much we can do. We will of course continue the investigation, but as far as your personal safety is concerned, well I don't know what to say other than be careful." He left the room, the young constable following in his wake.

Anne looked at PC Ridley, who had returned to her seat by the door. "Is it okay if I take a shower?" she asked. "The bathroom is down the hall."

"Of course," answered the constable, rising from her chair. "I'll wait outside the door."

"Is that really necessary?"

The constable fixed Anne with her direct blue eyes. "Well, that depends of course on who attacked you. If the attack was just a random incident, some trespasser, then no, protecting you is not necessary." She briefly dropped her gaze to the floor. "It's up to you, but in your place I would go see this Inspector Beckett in London. Tell her everything you know. She'll do her best to help you. It's her job."

"But what if I don't know anything?" asked Anne.

"Then tell her everything you guess."

Chapter Eight

ANNE COULDN'T BELIEVE what she was about to do. It was unthinkable. It was wrong. It had flashed into her mind at three a.m. the night before and stuck there like a tick on a dog, burrowing deeper and deeper until removal was impossible.

But it was a workable idea, she told herself now as she sat in her office, nervously tapping a pencil against her desk. A workable idea – maybe. But not a good one. Someone could get hurt – someone other than herself. The guilt just wasn't worth it.

She set the pencil down on her desk with exaggerated care and headed for the reception area. It was a quiet morning, and no clients were waiting. An anemic ray of London sunshine picked out a coffee stain on the industrial-blue carpet. Lindsey was flipping through Vogue and making small cooing noises at a spread on Valentino evening dresses.

"Hi Lindsey."

"Hi yourself, Anne. How's the arm?" Lindsey nodded at Anne's left arm, which was sporting a new, whiter-than-white cast.

"It's okay. It kind of itches. The A&E doctor said that's a good sign. Means it's healing."

"That's great." Lindsey flashed her a friendly smile, her teeth glowing brightly. Lindsey was wearing a rose-colored silk dress which made her look more innocent and less sexy than usual. It also made her look younger than her twenty-five years, which served to increase

Anne's guilt exponentially.

"Lindsey, could I ask you a favor?" Don't do it! her conscience screamed at her.

"Of course," Lindsey said, looking puzzled.

"I need you to take this guy out to lunch. Tomorrow. Between twelve and one-thirty."

Lindsey stared at her. Her mouth opened, then shut again. "Why?" she finally asked.

"It's . . . well. . ."

"It's important," Lindsey said quietly.

"Yes."

"This is none of my business – and I'll be happy to help, by the way – but does this have something to do with that car that hit you?"

"Maybe. That's what I'm trying to find out. I need to get this guy out of his office for an hour. So I can do a little . . . research."

"This guy, is he the one who hit you?"

"I don't know," Anne answered honestly. "But I need to find out."

"I see." A small worry line appeared in the middle of Lindsey's normally placid forehead. "I have to admit, I didn't care much for the guy when he was here. Twitchy little bugger, and definitely a cokehead."

"Oh. No. That was Daniel Soames, the owner of the car. This is . . . someone else."

ANNE WRAPPED HER parka around her more tightly. It wasn't cold outside, but she was shivering anyway. She leaned against a rough brick wall, watching the front door of Austin Friars House through the wrought-iron gate of the alley. She had double checked the clinic's schedule last night – it was posted on their web page. Dr. Davidson's two colleagues were not in the office on Tuesdays. The reason was not given and Anne didn't care. As long as they were gone. Mrs. Reed was an obstacle, but not an insurmountable one. Anne was pretty sure she could get past the receptionist. Mrs. Reed would go into that small kitchen behind her desk at some point during her lunch hour.

That only left Dr. Davidson. Anne checked her watch impatiently. It was fifteen minutes after twelve. Office workers had been straggling out of the building since noon. Lindsey had gone in at 12:05. It had been Lindsey's idea to chat up the security guard. She would flirt a little, act embarrassed, and confess to the guard that she had a crush on a cute guy with white-blond hair who she had seen coming out of Austin Friars House. The guard would wave Dr. Davidson over when he came down for lunch, introductions would follow, and Lindsey would whisk the doctor away to Chez Gerard on Bishopsgate.

Anne jumped as a group of suits walked by the mouth of the alley. If she stayed there much longer someone was going to report her to the police. She scrabbled in her pocket for a tissue and blew her nose, resisting the urge to check her watch again. A flash of turquoise caught her eye. Finally. Lindsey's dress today was a clingy silk wrap-around with a front slit in the skirt which came up so high it barely qualified as business appropriate. Anne had never seen her wear it in the office before, and guessed that it had been brought out specially for today's mission.

Dr. Davidson was clad in a precision-tailored cashmere overcoat. He was carrying a black trenchcoat. Lindsey paused at the top of the steps and held out an arm. The doctor helped her into the coat, his hands lingering just a touch too long on her shoulders. Anne winced. She could feel the guilt welling up. She wondered again if the doctor knew where she worked. If he'd ever gone up to their office. If he'd ever seen Lindsey.

Too late for second thoughts now. Lindsey and the doctor had disappeared. Anne took a deep breath and slipped through the wrought-iron gate and darted across the street. She pushed through the door of Austin Friars House and nodded at the guard in the blue blazer who was sitting behind the reception desk flipping through Tatler. Anne took the stairs. Memories of the building's ancient, creaking lift were vivid from her first visit. The last thing she needed was to get stuck in the lift.

She ran up the stairs two at a time. At the exit to the second floor she paused, listening. A group of women passed on the other side of the door, giggling about Prince William. Anne waited until she heard the lift doors close on them, then quietly slipped through the door and trotted down the hall. She preferred not to meet anyone if she could help it. It was a public building, no one would question her right to be there, but she didn't want word getting back to Dr. Davidson.

Anne stopped next to the dusty ficus which stood guard at the clinic's door. No sound came from within. She leaned casually against the wall and folded her arms. She wondered how long she could hang out in the hall before attracting attention.

A delicate cough sounded behind her. Anne jumped, then realized that the noise had come from within the clinic. Mrs. Reed. It sounded like the receptionist was at her desk. Paper was shuffled, a chair squeaked, and then ... ding. A microwave announced that it had finished the important task of heating Mrs. Reed's lunch.

Anne waited for the signal – dishes rattling in the kitchen. There. She held her breath and cautiously poked her head around the door. The reception area was empty. Resisting the temptation to run, she slunk past Mrs. Reed's desk and into the short hallway which ran down the center of the clinic. Dr. Davidson's elegantly decorated office was to her right, but she went past it. She glanced through a door to her left. Another office. Not what she was looking for. At the end of the hall she paused next to a closed door. Despite her caution a loud click sounded when she turned the handle. She froze. The noises coming from the kitchen had ceased. Don't just stand there, you idiot, Anne told herself frantically. Hide!

She shoved open the door and jumped inside, closing the door behind her. She put her ear against it. Footsteps would be hard to hear on the plush carpet of the clinic. She looked around for a hiding place. She was in a low-ceilinged room, about twelve feet by six, full of filing cabinets. A grimy window let in a weak stream of daylight. A table with boxes of loose folders underneath it was pushed against the wall. Anne crawled under this and pulled the boxes in front of her. Her shoulders hunched with tension as she waited. And waited.

Nothing. The door didn't burst open and disgorge Mrs. Reed at the head of the entire Bishopsgate police station. Anne took a deep breath and crawled sheepishly out from under the table. She tried to ignore her shaking hands and turned her attention to the filing cabinets. The drawers weren't marked so she tried one at random. It was filled with pens, pads of paper, post-its, and an empty can of Pringles – Original Flavor. The drawer above it was empty of everything except dustballs. Anne sighed and tried a drawer two cabinets over. It wouldn't open. She tugged at it without success. Locked. As were all the rest of the drawers. Her shoulders sagged and she looked behind her at the door to the hallway. She'd have to find the keys.

She glanced at her watch. 12:25. At most she had an hour left. Forty-five minutes to be on the safe side. Lindsey had promised to drag the lunch out as much as possible, but there was only so much stalling she could do before starting to look suspicious.

Anne eased open the door of the filing room. The click as the handle turned was barely audible this time. No one was in the hall, though she could hear Mrs. Reed talking on the phone at her desk. Leaving the filing room door open a crack, she crept to Dr. Davidson's office and slipped inside. She was tempted to close his door but knew that would be a mistake. Mrs. Reed was sure to notice the closed door if she happened to come into the hall.

The sculpted pine desk in the center of the room seemed the most logical choice. Anne crouched down behind it and eased open its only drawer – a long shallow one which ran the width of the desk. A Mont Blanc pen. Typical, Anne thought, and mentally rolled her eyes. Nothing else occupied the drawer except a blank pad of paper. Damn. She glanced around quickly. As it had on her first visit, the lack of office equipment struck her. The room more closely resembled a nineteenth-century drawing room than a psychiatrist's office. If Mrs. Reed had the only set of keys to the filing cabinets then she was stuck. That didn't seem likely though. Dr. Davidson was not the sort to give away all control like that. Of course, it was possible that he took the keys with him when he left the office, but Anne didn't think this was the case. A bulky set of office keys would ruin the precise line of his expensive suits.

Anne flopped down on the chair behind the desk with a discouraged sigh. 12:30. The overture of La Boheme floated into the room. Mrs. Reed was listening to the radio. Anne was tempted to give up. She still had to face the difficulty of getting past the receptionist and out of the clinic. She gazed absently at the desk in front of her. The curved pine legs were fashioned in a heavy modern style and were almost a foot wide at the top. Her eyes lighted on a faint line cut into the wood. At first its significance didn't register, but then she realized that the line traced a rectangle. A drawer was built into the leg of the desk. There was no handle. Anne pushed on the leg experimentally. Nope. She tried another spot. There. A tiny spring-loaded drawer ejected from its hiding place. Hidden drawers were a bit melodramatic, even for Dr. Davidson, thought Anne, but then realized that the drawer was most likely hidden so that it didn't spoil the lines of the sculpted desk and not from any nefarious purpose.

She got to her feet and bent over the drawer. A set of keys on a plain silver ring nestled on its bottom. Anne carefully pulled them out, squishing them together in her fist to prevent clinking. She closed the drawer and padded to the door. Mrs. Reed was singing quietly along with 'O soave fanciulla'. Anne dashed across the hall and shut herself in the filing room again. She relaxed slightly. It was unlikely that either Mrs. Reed or the psychiatrists came into this room on a daily basis.

She selected one of the smaller keys from the ring and tried it in the locked drawer she had chosen earlier. The key didn't fit. There were seven unlabeled keys in the set, five of which looked small enough to fit the cabinet drawers. 12:40. Anne exhaled impatiently and tried the next key. Then the next. Finally. She yanked open the drawer. Files of varying fullness were labeled Anderson, Bakely, Broughton . . . She moved to the right and selected a drawer in the last cabinet. Piper, Packard, Roberts.

Soames was in the next drawer she chose. Anne pulled out the file. It was nearly six inches wide and stuffed to capacity, its bottom worn through in places, sheets of paper poking through the holes. She laid it on the table she had hidden under and pulled out its contents, careful to keep the papers in order. There wasn't time to read each sheet. Most were invoices. She skipped over these, thumbing through the stack as fast as she could. There were pages of typed notes which she skimmed but didn't linger over. Anne guessed that Mrs. Reed had typed these up from the doctor's notes. He would be careful about what he let the receptionist see. She flipped through the sheets until she found a handwritten note.

'Jimmy spent entire session comparing Jameson whiskey to Jack Daniels. The Irish ended in the lead.'

Ok. Not particularly helpful. Anne flipped through to the next scrawled note.

'J.S. rehashed his school days. Wyndham becoming an obsession.'

This was more like it, but the lack of detail was disappointing. What she needed was a note in Dr. Davidson's handwriting stating that he was blackmailing James Soames. The note should of course be signed by the doctor and notarized by two witnesses. Anne sighed and checked her watch. 1:10. Damn. She was running out of time. She started flipping faster. Too fast. She almost missed it. It was stuck between two invoices and covered in doodles. Precise, geometric doodles of interlocking squares and triangles.

'J.S. harping on incident again. The boy had it coming, not J's fault, etc, etc. Tired of this obsession, no matter how useful.'

Anne read it again and then laid it to one side. It was suggestive, but it was not enough. She thought of the anonymous note slipped into her mailbox. That had mentioned Wyndham Preparatory. That letter combined with this note might have been enough to take to the police. If only she hadn't handed it over to Dr. Davidson. Aargh. Now she needed more. For a brief moment she let herself hope that the doctor might have tucked the note somewhere in Jimmy's folder, but reality quickly squashed that idea. To keep the note would have been both stupid and careless. The doctor was neither. He gave the impression that every detail of his life was carefully planned and even more carefully executed.

Anne scanned the remaining handwritten notes in the folder but nothing else useful turned up. She folded the note she had set aside and tucked it into the pocket of her jeans. She carefully returned the papers to their folder and tucked 'Soames, James' back into its place behind 'Sanderson, William'. With the cabinet locked and the keys in her pocket Anne prepared herself for the trials to come. Don't think too much about it, she told herself. First return the keys, then get past Mrs. Reed. Keys, then Mrs. Reed. She took a deep breath, flexed her shaking hands, and reached for the doorknob.

"Good afternoon Miss Stewart. The doctor is out to lunch at the moment, but he should be back any second. You're just a few minutes early."

Anne didn't hear Miss Stewart's reply. She didn't need to. It was obvious who Miss Stewart was. One of Dr. Davidson's patients. Calmly seating herself in the reception area, blocking escape.

Anne leaned her head against the door and whimpered. No, no, no. She froze there, unable to move. She was rapidly losing her nerve. The temptation to throw open the door and run out of the clinic in full view of Mrs. Reed and the inconvenient Miss Stewart was irresistible. Her hand grasped the doorknob and turned it.

"Mrs. Reed would you mail another invoice to Mr. Perry. His payment is late again. Hello Miss Stewart. Come right in."

Anne jerked her hand off the doorknob as if it was red hot. The doctor was back. She looked around in panic, but the choice of hiding places hadn't changed. She threw herself under the table and pulled the boxes of files in front of her. She crouched down until she was curled into a ball on the floor. A small dust cloud floated up and into her nose. She pinched her nostrils together, and bit her lip for good measure. Then she listened.

"No, I've never eaten there," Miss Stewart said. "I hear it's nice."

The doctor's answer was too low to be heard. They must have gone into his office, Anne thought. Thank god she had closed that desk drawer. She listened desperately for the sound of a door closing, but it didn't come. The doctor's desk faced the door of his office. The open door. There was no way she could get by.

4:50 P.M. THE square of sky framed by the window of the filing room was nearly black. A sliver of light from the hall showed under the door. Anne yawned and stretched out her legs, bumping against a filing cabinet. She couldn't remember the moment which just passed and realized that she must have fallen asleep. Something had woken her. She raised her head and peeked over the boxes in front of her. No one was in the room with her. She heard a door shut.

"Don't worry doctor. I'll lock up. I'm so happy you had a good time at lunch. It's about time you had a young lady in your life. You have a good evening."

Dr. Davidson was going home already. Anne wasn't surprised. He had never struck her as a person who would keep long hours.

Blackmail was undoubtedly more profitable than hard work.

The sound of clinking dishes came through the wall. Mrs. Reed doing the final wash up of the day. A few minutes of silence followed during which Anne couldn't tell what the occupants of the clinic were doing. She was reasonably sure that the doctor had left. Mrs. Reed was no longer chatting to him anyway, and the receptionist struck her as one of those people who couldn't help talking if there was someone around to hear her.

A door closed, followed by the sound of a bolt turning in its lock. The clinic's outer door had been shut and locked. Anne crawled out from her hiding place and dusted herself off. She double checked the cabinet drawers to make sure she had locked them all, then crept to the door and eased it open. The hallway was dark. Thank god. The escapade was almost over. A sense of frustration welled up inside her. All this effort, not to mention her shattered nerves, and not much to show for it. Well, you can't do anything about that now, Anne told herself firmly as she went into Dr. Davidson's office and returned the keys to their drawer.

She felt her way down the hall and across the reception area. It was so dark that it was difficult to see. She paused in front of the outer door. She was no expert, but there didn't appear to be any alarm system. No small boxes with blinking lights on the wall near the door. Of course, there might be an alarm box on the other side of the door. Anne racked her brain, but couldn't remember whether there was one or not. She'd have to chance it. She grasped the door handle and turned. It caught on something, and for one panicked moment the thought flashed through her mind that she was locked inside the clinic. But a second turn to the handle released the bolt. Anne slumped in relief. She pulled the door open a crack. No one was in the hall. She could hear voices, but they sounded hollow and far away. Most likely people in the lift, going down to the lobby and home for the day. She pulled the door open farther. What was that smell? It reminded her of anti-freeze, or ice cubes. Shit!

Anne tried to dodge around him but he was blocking the doorway. He grabbed her arm up near the shoulder and pushed her back into the clinic. The overhead lights were switched on and Anne blinked from the glare. He dragged her with him as he strode to Mrs. Reed's desk and picked up the phone.

"Hello, Robert. This is Dr. Davidson from the psychiatric clinic on the second floor. I've had a break-in. Please call the police. Thank you."

Anne tried to twist away from him but he tightened his grasp until he was just short of leaving a bruise.

"Well," he said. "This is unexpected." He stared at her with an expression Anne couldn't quite understand. It was the face of someone who'd just had a stroke of luck. "I suppose I should ask the obvious question – what are you doing here?"

Ok, Anne thought. This was where she came up with a brilliant reason for her presence. So brilliant that he was completely taken in, let her go, cancelled the call to the police, and left her free to trot off home and indulge in a much needed bowl of macaroni and cheese.

Sigh. She stared woodenly at the floor and didn't answer him.

Running footsteps sounded in the hall and then a chunky white guy in a blazer that strained against his pot belly burst into the room. Anne didn't recognize him. The guy who'd been at the guard desk in the lobby when she entered the building had been an older black guy.

"You (gasp) ok (gasp) doctor?" The guard had obviously run up the stairs and just as obviously was not accustomed to such activity.

"I'm fine," snapped Dr. Davidson. "Did you call the police?"

"Yes sir. I called the Bishopsgate station as it's the closest. They said someone will be here in about ten minutes. I hope that's ok. I didn't call 999 as a break-in didn't seem like an emergency." He stopped and looked at Anne, his expression relaxing. Finding that the perpetrator was a small woman who was shaking from head to toe seemed to justify his assessment of the situation as a non-emergency.

The doctor nodded. "Thank you Robert. Go down and wait for the police."

"Right." Robert trundled out, the floor groaning at each step.

Anne missed him already. She was alone with the doctor again, and an insistent bubble of fear for her safety was growing. She told herself not to be stupid – he wouldn't do anything with the police on the way. His personality also worked in her favor. She'd be in more danger if he was hot-tempered and easy to incite. A person like that might forget possible consequences in the heat of the moment and strike out. But even her limited contact with the doctor had shown her he wasn't like that. Calculated self-interest governed his actions, and violence was not in his best interest right now.

He was still gripping her arm, even though there was no longer any real need. She was hardly going to run away at this point. It would make her look even more guilty in the eyes of the police. Anne came to the unsettling conclusion that he was still holding her because he enjoyed it. She tried to convince herself that it was just that he enjoyed causing pain – which was probably true. Her subconscious, however, had detected a sexual subtext to his behavior and it was dutifully bringing this to her attention. Anne shuddered.

Dr. Davidson smiled, his thin lips not quite parting. "What are you going to tell the police?"

"What?" asked Anne in surprise.

"You obviously snuck in here in order to snoop around, but you can hardly tell the police that. I was just curious as to what excuse you'd come up with."

"I don't know." Anne shrugged hopelessly. "I can't think of anything plausible."

Dr. Davidson chuckled, his transparent eyes gleaming with amusement – or lust. Anne didn't want to know which.

"Let go already," she spat, twisting and squirming in frustration.

He let her struggle for a few moments, then seemed to tire of the game. He marched her over to a chair and pushed her into it, then sat down in a chair farther away from the door, as if daring her to make a run for it.

They sat there silently, the doctor watching Anne and Anne watching the door. When the two uniformed police officers arrived she jumped up as if standing to attention. The doctor stood more leisurely.

"Thank you for coming officers," he said calmly. "I found this young lady in the clinic – the locked clinic – after I and my staff had left for the day. I caught her when I returned to pick up some papers I had forgotten."

The officers looked at Anne without interest. It was obvious that they didn't consider her much of a threat to public safety. The older man spoke up.

"Do you want to press charges sir?"

"Yes, I do."

The officer looked surprised at this, but shrugged and proceeded to read Anne her rights.

Chapter Nine

IT HAD BEEN a long night. Anne yawned and flexed her left arm, which had gone numb. She'd fallen asleep sitting up, her arm squashed against the bars of the cell. Her cellmate was still snoring gently, the purple spandex of her miniskirt twisted around her hefty thighs.

Anne tried to guess what time it was. The noise coming from the front of the police station had increased considerably in the last half hour. It must be close to normal business hours, maybe 8:00 a.m. Her stomach growled loudly. She wondered if they would feed her. They hadn't bothered last night, just chucked her in here and left.

Heels clacked on the dirty tile floor, coming toward her cell. Anne leaned toward the noise, wondering if she had a visitor. The person who came into view was Inspector Beckett, her blue suit and gray bob remaining immobile as she walked, as if both were cut from the same unbendable fabric. DC Singh was not with her this time.

"Good Morning, Miss Lambert. I hope you slept well."

Anne decided this was ironic and didn't respond.

"I have an interview room waiting. Would you come with me please." She unlocked the cell door and held it open.

Anne stood up stiffly and waited in the passage while the Inspector re-locked the cell. Her cellmate snorted as the metal door clanged, but didn't wake. Inspector Beckett led the way up the chewing-gum speckled hallway to the front of the station. Business was slow this time of day. A uniformed officer, engrossed in coffee and paperwork, hunched over a wooden counter which took up half the room. He didn't glance up as Inspector Beckett deposited the cell keys in front of him.

She motioned Anne to follow her. They wandered through a maze of narrow hallways and cubicles, finally stopping at a small room which had a clipboard hanging from its door. The Inspector checked her watch, wrote the time on the clipboard, then waved Anne into the room, closing the door behind them. A scarred wooden table and two metal chairs were the only things inside.

"Please sit down."

Anne pulled out a chair, a metallic scrape echoing off the walls. She sat down warily and watched as the Inspector flipped through a file she had brought with her.

"First, let me say that this is an off-the-record interview, an informal chat if you will. I'm not taping it." The Inspector leaned toward Anne, her gray bob swinging forward in one over-hairsprayed mass, her hazel eyes intent. She seemed to be waiting for Anne to respond. Anne nodded cautiously to show she understood. The Inspector relaxed back into her chair.

"Let's start with the good news. Dr. John Davidson has decided not to press charges against you. This means, of course, that we have no reason to hold you. You are free to go, but it would be to your benefit to wait and hear me out. There are some things we need to discuss." She paused again and Anne nodded.

"An Inspector Northam called me yesterday. He told me about your little adventure in Kent. Attempted drowning, of all things. That makes two attempts on your life in less than a month."

Her expression was disapproving. Anne got the feeling that in the Inspector's opinion respectable people were not the targets of attempted murder. Certainly not repeated attempts, anyway. Anne decided to ignore the implied criticism. The Inspector's last remark had caught her attention.

"Two attempts. So that car which hit me – you have proof that it wasn't an accident?"

"Proof? No, I wouldn't go that far," the Inspector admitted. "What we have are several witness statements which all agree that the car didn't slow or attempt to swerve before it hit you. Nothing hid you from the view of the driver. You were right in the middle of the street. But it's not so much the details of the accident itself as the owner of the car which I find interesting. It's quite a coincidence that the owner, Daniel Soames, should have a brother who drowned only a week before your accident. And then you turn out to be the neighbor of this brother's psychiatrist. And now we find you poking around the psychiatrist's office." She stopped and looked at Anne pointedly.

Anne dropped her eyes to the table in front of her. "Carl sucks!" was scratched into the wood next to a rather artistically drawn pig with a curly tail. She traced the pig with her finger. They sat in silence, the minutes ticking away uncomfortably. Finally, to break the tension more than anything else, Anne reached into the front pocket of her jeans and pulled out a crumpled scrap of paper. She pushed this across the table.

The Inspector opened it and read it aloud.

"J.S. harping on incident again. The boy had it coming, not J's fault, etc, etc. Tired of this obsession, no matter how useful."

She frowned at Anne. "Where did you get this?"

"From the file on James Soames, in Dr. Davidson's office."

The Inspector's frown deepened to two grooves extending halfway up her forehead. "So this is what you were looking for when you broke in there."

"I didn't break in," Anne said defensively. "I just slipped in at lunch time – the clinic was open for business – and hid in the filing room."

"You're splitting hairs and you know it."

"Maybe," admitted Anne, "but I was desperate."

"The attempts on your life. Yes, I can see how you'd feel that way. What I don't understand is why you didn't come talk to me sooner. You knew I was already investigating Daniel Soames."

"That's the problem. You're investigating Daniel Soames for his brother's murder. Okay, fine. But that doesn't help me." Anne tapped the note with a finger. "J.S. is James Soames. Dr. Davidson's patient. I think the boy referred to in this note was a Wyndham Preparatory student who was strangled at the school about fifteen years ago. Strangled by James Soames. Dr. Davidson was the school's guidance counselor at the time. He spent a lot of time counseling James, and I think James confessed to the killing, probably during one of their sessions. I think the doctor has been blackmailing James ever since. Now, Daniel Soames may have killed his brother. I don't know and I don't care. Daniel has a petty little grudge against me because I wouldn't help him retrieve his car after the police impounded it, but that's all. I don't think Daniel has it in for me. But someone else does – two attempts on my life, after all. And I'm beginning to suspect that person is Dr. Davidson."

The Inspector had remained silent throughout this speech, watching Anne carefully and fingering a gold chain which hung down over her jacket. When Anne finished she read the note again and then stared off into space for several minutes, her face expressionless.

Finally she returned her attention to Anne. "I take it you didn't deduce all of that from this note," she said, the sarcasm unmistakable.

"No, of course not. I heard about the boy who was killed from a teacher at Wyndham Preparatory. The teacher's first name is Kenneth. I don't remember his surname."

Anne watched as the Inspector took a small notebook out of her jacket pocket and made a note in it. Anne found this oddly comforting, probably because someone was taking her suspicions seriously.

"Is there anything else?" asked Inspector Beckett.

Anne looked at her doubtfully, but realized that she may as well finish what she'd started. "There was another note, handwritten, which was left in my mailbox. I don't have it anymore. I gave it to Dr. Davidson."

The Inspector's eyebrows went up at this.

"I know, I know," said Anne. "It was a stupid thing to do. But I didn't suspect him of anything at that point. I felt sorry for him. The note seemed to indicate that someone had a grudge against him. I felt obligated to let him know about it."

"Can you remember what the note said?"

"Sure. It was only a few lines, plus I have a good memory." Anne quoted:

"I just wanted you to know who you're living next door to. He's hurt a lot of people. He got to me years ago. At school. Wyndham Prep. Ask him about Wyndham Prep."

"Hmm," said the Inspector noncommittally. "Write it down please. Word for word." She pushed her notebook and pen across the table. "You realize that your suspicions of the doctor are pretty flimsy. You have no solid evidence of any wrong doing."

"I know that. That's why I haven't talked to the police."

"Well, I'll try to keep an open mind, but there's nothing I can do without something more solid. We've already talked to the doctor in his role as James Soames' psychiatrist. It would be difficult to bring him in for another chat as things stand. I have the feeling he's the type who would be quick to claim police harassment. Daniel Soames is another matter. He's still our main suspect for the two attempts on your life. The car which hit you was owned by him, and someone tried to drown you while you were a guest at his parent's home. Plus Inspector Northam mentioned the shoe prints they've collected which matched a pair of Soames' shoes. This is the kind of evidence the courts like – simple and physical. And in the other matter of James Soames' death, the evidence there also points to Daniel Soames.

Daniel is the second son in a very wealthy family. He inherited when his brother died. There's no physical evidence to link him to James' death, but there is certainly a motive."

The Inspector paused to fish a business card out of her pocket. "Here's my card. Call me if anything else happens. Hopefully it won't. Daniel Soames knows we're watching him, and I'll make some discreet inquiries about Dr. Davidson. I can't promise anything, though. If I were you, I'd keep an eye out when crossing the street."

Chapter Ten

WHEN ANNE ENTERED the office the next day Lindsey jumped up.

"Anne! Where have you been? I've been so worried. You went into that building on Austin Friars Street and never came out again. After we got back from lunch I waited for you outside for more than an hour. I finally had to leave because people were starting to look at me strangely. One jerk had the nerve to ask what my rates were." Lindsey's elegant features scrunched up in distaste.

Anne took a quick look down the hall. No one else was around. She motioned Lindsey over to the reception area's chairs.

"I'm sorry Lindsey. I should have called you. I'll tell you what happened, but I need you to promise that you won't tell anyone else. It's not the kind of thing I want people at work to know."

"Of course I won't talk about it, if that's what you want," said Lindsey, a vertical frown line breaking through her normally placid expression.

"I was arrested."

Lindsey's blue eyes widened but she didn't say anything.

"You can see why I don't want my boss to know. The charges were dropped, so there's no permanent blot on my record, as far as I know. I'm not sure how these things work. Still, as a foreign national, getting myself arrested could be a problem. I could lose my work permit."

"Oh, surely not. I'm sure The Franklin Group wouldn't do that. Not if you explained the circumstances. Plus, you've worked for them for quite a while now. How long did you work for them in Los Angeles?"

"Five years."

"See. You're a valued employee."

"You're probably right, but for now I think it will be easier to just not mention this whole episode to them. Okay?"

"Of course. Whatever you want. Now, come on. Spill. What happened?"

"Dr. Davidson caught me in his office. He came back for something, and returned right when I was trying to sneak out of the clinic. He called the police and had me arrested for breaking and entering, or whatever you call it here. I spent the night in a cell, then found out the next day that he'd dropped the charges. I have the feeling that he never intended to take the matter all the way to court. He just wanted to scare me."

"Really?" asked Lindsey doubtfully. "Why would he do that? He seems like such a nice person."

Anne stared at her. "A nice person? You're kidding, right?"

"Not at all," said Lindsey in surprise. "He was a perfect gentleman at lunch. Very polite and attentive. Actually, I'm thinking of seeing him again. He asked me to that Jose Carreras recital at the Barbican."

Anne's mouth fell open in disbelief. Her dislike of the doctor had been so strong, right from the first moment they'd met, that she found it impossible to imagine that someone else could actually like him.

"You didn't tell him where you worked did you?" asked Anne, trying to keep her voice calm.

"No, of course not. Give me some credit please. He doesn't know we work in the same office. I just said that I work near his clinic on Austin Friars, and that I'd seen him several times at that Pret A Manger on Old Broad street. He told me that he buys his lunch there most days, so it seemed like a plausible story. Anyway, I don't give out any personal details like address or phone numbers on a first date."

"It wasn't a date," said Anne in exasperation. "It was a diversion."

"Well, yes. I know. But it turns out that we enjoyed each other's company. He's the kind I go for. Older, sophisticated, with possible sugar-daddy potential."

"Lindsey!"

Lindsey grinned at her impishly. "Oh, don't look so shocked. I know you love your career, and I think that's great. You're very good at it. But I've never been that fond of working. I'd much prefer to be kept. Kept and married, hopefully, but I'm flexible."

Anne dropped her head into her hands and yanked on her hair.

"Oh, come on. It's not that bad." Lindsey patted her on the shoulder. "I promise I'll be careful. I know you don't like him, but I honestly don't think he's involved in that hit-and-run business of yours. If you ask me, that awful Soames person who showed up here is the one you should be worried about."

AT HER DESK, Anne reflected that both Lindsey and Inspector Beckett thought Daniel Soames was the person she should be careful of. She stirred more sugar into her tea and forced herself to think about this idea objectively. She didn't like Daniel, in fact she found him repulsive, but she had instinctively considered him less of a threat than Dr. Davidson. Right from the start. Why?

Her train of thought was broken by Nick, who bounded into the room and threw his backpack on his desk.

"Dudette, where've you been?"

"Um, sick. Just a cold. Why? Are we slipping on our Barclay's deadline?"

"Nah. Nothing like that. Everything's cool. I just wondered. Hey, did Lindsey tell you that I covered the switchboard for her on Tuesday? It was sweet. Her phone has ten lines. Ten! I think I transferred one poor dude to China. It's a serious juggling act up there. Two lines rang at the same time and I was like sweating. I mean, which do you answer first? You want to be democratic and all that, you know, first come first served, but it's tough when two of those little buttons light up at the same time. Major dilemma. I finally closed my eyes and punched at random. Of course, I missed the phone entirely the first couple of times, but I eventually got those guys happily transferred. I'm like the god of phones now. Just call me phone guy."

"Great, phone guy. Now, why don't we get to work. I have a couple of stored procedures to write and I need to use those new Oracle tables you were creating. Are they done yet?"

Chapter Eleven

THE DOORBELL JARRED Anne out of a dream the next morning. Gonzo had banded together with Fozzie Bear, and their successful coup d'etat had deposed Kermit from the throne of England. The Queen Mother was shell-shocked. As was Anne. Was she destined to spend the rest of her life dreaming about the Muppets?

She stumbled to the door, pulling on her bathrobe. "Who is it?" she asked the door grumpily.

"Carstairs Miss."

Huh? Who the heck was Carstairs? Reluctantly Anne opened the door. The man standing in the hallway was wearing an elegantly tailored chauffeur's costume, his gray hair rumpled from the hat he held in his hands. Oh, right. Carstairs. Lady Soames' butler. Anne frowned at him in confusion.

"Um, Hi. What are you doing here?"

"Lady Soames has requested that I collect you Miss. She is at the family's London home, near Regents Park, and would like to speak with you. Now, if that would be convenient." Carstairs had the grace to look embarrassed at his employer's extremely abrupt summons.

"Um, okay," said Anne, rather taken aback. "I guess that would be all right. It's Saturday, so I don't have to go into the office. Come on in. Did Lady Soames say what this is about?"

"No Miss," said Carstairs apologetically. "Her Ladyship can be uninformative at times."

Anne sighed and bowed to the inevitable. "Okay. Have a seat." She waved vaguely in the direction of the sofa. "I'll just get changed." She left Carstairs sitting quietly, his hat on his knees, and closed the door behind her as she went into the bedroom. She splashed water on her face, then pulled on her usual jeans and t-shirt, mentally cursing herself as she stepped into her Nikes. She had to learn how to say no to people. Maybe there was a course she could take. How to stand up for yourself in three easy lessons. Of course, even a master of the art would find it difficult to stand up to Lady Soames.

"Okay, I'm as ready as I'll ever be," she said, coming out of the bedroom. "Could you hand me my coat?"

Carstairs looked confused by this request, until he spotted the forest green parka lying on the floor at his feet. He plucked it up and politely helped Anne into it. Anne grabbed her purse off the kitchen table and ushered him out, locking the door carefully behind them.

"Anne dear!" Mrs. Watson rushed down the hall towards them, trailing blue paper streamers. Silver confetti was scattered across her shoulders like sparkly dandruff. "Just the person I wanted to see. Georgie is having his birthday tomorrow. He's going to be three!" She paused to give them time to take in this spectacular achievement. "I'm having the party here – his mother had some ludicrous idea about the zoo – and I need a second opinion on the decorations. I'm afraid they may not be sophisticated enough for a child of Georgie's taste and discernment. You must help me. Your friend can come too."

"Uh . . . " As usual, Anne was finding it difficult to come up with an excuse which would foil Mrs. Watson. Mrs. Watson was leading her down the hall by her arm when Carstairs broke in.

"Madam," he said smoothly, "I'm afraid we will not be able to assist you at present. Miss Lambert has an urgent meeting to attend. I'm sure you understand." He gently removed Anne's arm from Mrs. Watson's grip and steered her around the streamers.

"Carstairs, I think I love you," said Anne.

Carstairs took this in stride. "Thank you Miss. As you might expect, I have extensive experience coping with elderly ladies of an imperious nature. I've found that an element of surprise combined with a quick exit works in most situations." His gray eyes twinkled at her. "If I may make a suggestion Miss – you need to work on your speed. Always present a moving target. Don't freeze like a deer in headlights."

IT WAS A nice day, for March. A pale sun was shining on the leafless maples in Tavistock Square, lighting up the crocuses at their roots like votive candles. As they drove through Bloomsbury Anne settled back into the squashy leather seat. Lady Soames' London car was a Rolls – a Silver Ghost. A bit of a cliché, admittedly, but an impressive cliché. It was a new experience for Anne, being chauffeured through London's crowded streets in the back of a Rolls Royce. She decided to enjoy the ride no matter what lay ahead. She rolled the window down and stuck her head out, squinting her eyes against the rush of wind. Other drivers swiveled as they passed, checking out the Rolls. Anne couldn't decide if this was flattering or embarrassing. She finally decided on the latter and pulled her head back inside.

The car turned onto Outer Circle Drive, skirting the Regents Park lake, empty of rowboats this time of year. As they drove by Anne watched two large spotted geese waddle out of the lake and converge on a toddler who was hesitantly offering a piece of bread. The geese hissed as they came, their long necks undulating like twin cobras. The toddler looked like she was about to cry. She bravely stood her ground until the lead goose got to within six inches of her shaking hand, then she dropped the bread and ran. Very wise, Anne decided.

Turning a blind eye to geese and other dangers lurking in the park, Carstairs swung off the main drive and onto a side street marked Hanover Terrace. The driveway he pulled into circled in front of a cream-colored building more than a block long. The building proudly displayed its granite columns and pediment like the status symbols they were. Anne hopped out and paused to admire the building.

"John Nash?" she asked Carstairs, who had turned off the car and was standing beside her.

"Yes Miss. 1810. I especially like the frieze." He pointed to a large bas-relief over the columned entrance. White marble figures on a sky-blue background were lined up side-by-side as if queuing for a bus.

"Does the Soames family own this whole building?"

"No Miss. Not even the Queen herself owns one of these buildings in its entirety." He pointed to an octagonal tower halfway between the entrance and the end of the building. "The Soames family occupies that tower, as well as a large portion of the first floor. If you'll follow me please."

He led her under the columns and up immaculate marble steps into the entrance hall. Anne, who was expecting something grand and ballroomy, was disappointed. The carpet was Persian, and orchids sprouted from a vase by the door, but the overall impression was that of a Hilton reception area. A uniformed doorman was seated behind a polished wooden counter. Carstairs nodded at him and continued on to a stairway to their right. The Persian carpet of the hall continued up the stairs, held in place by heavy brass rods under each step. At the top of the stairs they turned down a long paneled hallway lined with doors, each of which had a shiny brass number on it. As they walked the doors got farther and farther apart. Anne guessed that the flats behind the doors were getting larger. At the end of the hall they turned into a kind of cul-de-sac which had only one door. Carstairs unlocked this and ushered Anne inside.

The room they entered was octagonal-shaped, with a brightly glowing chandelier suspended from its high ceiling. A cream-colored rug spilled across the floor, lilacs winding around its edge. The only furniture consisted of a Louis XVI mahogany side-table. Carstairs laid his keys on this and waved Anne towards a staircase which curved to fit the wall like a vine wrapping around a tree trunk. Anne guessed that they were ascending to the next floor of the tower Carstairs had pointed out. She could hear voices up ahead.

"Sit down Daniel," said Lady Soames' voice. "All that pacing is wearing on my nerves."

"Miss Lambert, Madam." Carstairs waved Anne inside and disappeared back down the stairs.

Anne paused awkwardly at the entrance to the room, uncomfortably aware of being stared at. The room was circular, with delicate Louis XVI furnishings grouped to face its center. Lady Soames and Dr. Davidson were ensconced on a window seat which followed the curve of the tower. Over their heads she could see the lake and the rest of Regents Park stretching away like a green carpet. Daniel was sprawled in a gilt-edged chair, his legs spread so widely it bordered on indecent behavior. Leaning against the far wall was a tall man with overly-long dark hair and a scraggly goatee. Anne frowned. She'd seen him somewhere before.

"Please sit down dear," said Lady Soames, gesturing regally toward a chair opposite Daniel. "Would you like some tea?" Without waiting for a response she poured from a silver teapot which rested on a damask-covered table in front of her. "Milk and sugar?"

"Just sugar, please."

Anne took the delicate bone china cup and saucer with the care of a bomb squad expert handling a suspicious package. She balanced on the edge of her chair and stirred her tea, waiting for someone to speak. Daniel was ignoring her. Lady Soames and Dr. Davidson exchanged a long look which suggested a conversation left unfinished. Lady Soames unconsciously smoothed the skirt of her teal silk dress with a repetitive motion, the gold bangles on her wrist clinking. To Anne's astonishment she appeared almost nervous.

Finally, Lady Soames began. "Miss Lambert, you are aware that my son James was killed not long ago. Drowned, near Greenwich."

Anne nodded, a vertical frown line growing between her eyes as she glanced from Lady Soames to Dr. Davidson. Lady Soames met her gaze with a face rigidly devoid of expression, but the doctor seemed amused by something. He busied himself adjusting the pale blue cuffs which extended a precise half-inch from under the sleeve of his jacket.

"I believe you knew James. When we talked at our family home in Kent you mentioned that you'd spoken to him several times, struck up an acquaintance."

"No," replied Anne cautiously, "I only met him once, very briefly, when he came to see Dr. Davidson."

"Really. I was under the impression that there was more to the acquaintance. Well, no matter. It's not so much the length of time you two spent together as what was said."

Anne stared at her, baffled. She couldn't for the life of her see where this was leading, but Lady Soames seemed to be following some kind of agenda. She spoke her words like a bad actress who hadn't memorized all of her lines.

"John – Dr. Davidson – and I feel certain that James must have confided in you."

"Confided?"

"Yes. Confided. Talked to you about certain friends of his. Unfortunately he had gotten mixed up with a rather rough group of people. Drugs, that kind of thing. We feel quite sure that someone in this group is responsible for his death. Our family would be grateful if you took it upon yourself to go to the police and tell them everything you know. You see, it would look better coming from someone outside the family. Someone like yourself, with no ulterior motive. If I were to contact the police they would assume that it was something I had fabricated in order to protect Daniel. Daniel, you see, has been arrested. Charged with his brother's murder. My husband and I posted his bail immediately, of course, but it has been an ordeal for all of us." Lady Soames turned to Dr. Davidson, who patted her hand and nodded consolingly.

Anne just stared at her. The conversation had taken on such an unreal quality that she had no idea how to respond. Lady Soames waited, her face back to its usual regal mask. Anne glanced over at Dr. Davidson. He was looking at her like a fisherman reeling in his catch. Light began to dawn. They didn't really think that Jimmy had told her anything. They just wanted to make use of her, to get Daniel off the hook. They expected her to go to the police and perjure herself. Anne was amazed that they had even considered it. Admittedly, Lady Soames was used to getting what she wanted, but this was ridiculous. They had no hold on her, nothing which could force her to do this.

"I appreciate that you're just trying to protect your son," Anne began cautiously, "but I can't do what you're asking. Jimmy never mentioned drugs, or discussed his friends with me."

"My dear," began Lady Soames, but stopped when Dr. Davidson placed a hand on her arm.

"Anne," he said smoothly, "I know this is a difficult thing we're asking, but think of all the people it will benefit – Daniel, Lady Soames, your friend Lindsey."

And the trap closed. She hadn't seen it, hiding in the grass, and now it was fastened on her leg, its metal teeth drawing blood. Dr. Davidson watched her with a hungry expression.

"Lindsey is a delight," he said softly. "We got along famously at lunch the other day. In fact, we're going out again next week. To a recital at the Barbican. Jose Carreras is singing. I'm picking her up at work. Perhaps I'll see you there."

Anne didn't reply. There was no point.

"Well," continued the doctor as he rose from his seat and adjusted his tie by a fraction of a millimeter, "I think we're finished here. Lady Soames, it's been a pleasure, as always." He bent and grasped her hand briefly. "Anne, why don't I see you out. Carstairs can give us both a ride home." He approached Anne as if to help her out of her chair, but she ignored him.

"Why did they arrest you?" she asked, looking straight at Daniel. He was so taken aback by the question that his face didn't have time to assume its usual petulant expression.

"The police found something in Greenwich, near where Jimmy was murdered," he grudgingly replied. "A marble paperweight from my desk at work. A model of the Bank of England. The old man . . ." Lady Soames frowned at him. ". . . my father gave it to me when I started my first job. It had my fingerprints all over it, and some of Jimmy's blood. They claim I hit him on the head with it and then dumped him in the river. I didn't, of course." The customary whine had returned to his voice. "I told them it must have been planted, but no one believes me."

"Planted by whom?" asked Anne.

"By whoever killed Jimmy, of course."

"Of course it was planted," Dr. Davidson broke in smoothly. "By one of Jimmy's drug-dealing friends. A point Anne can mention when she talks to the police. Now, we should be going. Lady Soames has other appointments to keep." He reached for Anne's arm, but she twitched away from him.

"Why wasn't it found before now?" she asked Daniel.

"What?" asked Daniel blankly.

Anne struggled with the impatience which every conversation with Daniel seemed to generate. It was like coping with an extremely spoiled, lazy child. She took a deep breath and tried again. "Why didn't the police find this paperweight weeks ago, when they first searched the crime scene?"

"How would I know?" snapped Daniel, as if the topic had nothing to do with him. "Because the police are fuckin' idiots, I expect."

"Daniel!" said Lady Soames sharply. She went over to him, hand raised. Anne expected her to give him a cuff on the head – he could certainly use one – but instead she smoothed down his hair. Daniel was not appreciative, and arched his back like an angry kitten. He launched himself from his chair and left the room in a huff. They could hear his footsteps echo along the stairway like a two-year old's temper-tantrum stomps.

Anne felt a chill in the room. She wasn't saying her lines correctly, and she could tell that Lady Soames and Dr. Davidson were wondering if they should have chosen another actress for the part.

"Miss Lambert," began Lady Soames, but was interrupted by the doctor, who raised his hand like a cop stopping traffic. He helped Anne from her chair with more force than gallantry and escorted her from the room. When they reached the entrance hall Carstairs materialized as if on cue.

"Shall I drive you back home Miss?"

"No thank you," said Anne, maneuvering so that Carstairs was between her and the doctor. "I think I'll take a walk through the park. It's a nice day for it."

"Now that is a shame," said Dr. Davidson as Carstairs helped him on with his overcoat. "I was hoping we could talk on the ride back. There are a few things I want to discuss with you, and I don't have time to feed the ducks. Ride back with me. You can go for a walk another time."

Anne crossed her arms, set for battle. She was about to reply when footsteps sounded on the stairs. Heavy black motorcycle boots appeared first, then grubby jeans and a black leather jacket – the long fringe on its sleeves brushing the banister like a horse's mane. As the man's face came into view Anne suddenly remembered where she'd seen him. It was the man in the snapshot. The one she'd found in the flat in Soho.

He clumped toward them, boots leaving bits of mud on the cream-colored rug. As he approached Anne noticed something silver dangling from his left ear. A razorblade.

"Hey, sweetness," he said, addressing Anne. "Did you get my note?"

Anne's mouth dropped open in surprise. "What note?" she managed to choke out.

The man scratched his scruffy goatee and winked at her. "The note I left in your mailbox, darling."

"Oh," Anne mouthed silently, suddenly keenly aware that Dr. Davidson was watching her.

"I was thinking maybe we could take a walk in the park, talk a few things over. Won't take long." He waited, a slight smirk on his face, as if expecting someone to object to this suggestion. Which they did.

"Miss Lambert, I really don't think you should . . ." burst out Carstairs.

The doctor chimed in with "Anne, this is not a person you should be associating with."

Anne waved them to silence. "I'm not wandering around the park with you. How about finding a café nearby, where we can talk."

"I don't do cafes, honey." A leather-clad arm threw itself around Anne's shoulders. "There's a pub down on Baker Street. The Slug and Lettuce. The glasses aren't too clean, but the Guinness is straight off the boat from Dublin."

"Fine," Anne spat out, throwing off his arm. She thanked Carstairs for her coat and led the way out the door.

ANNE SQUIRMED ON her barstool, peering with distaste at a copy of the pub's food-spattered menu. The front cover boasted a fat slug crawling across what appeared to be a moldy green washcloth – the beleaguered lettuce, presumably. The Slug and Lettuce plied its trade two doors down from the Sherlock Holmes museum, and its menu was geared toward the tourist. Lots of 'ye olde' and 'traditional'. 'Ye Olde Spotted Dick' was the highlight of the dessert section. Serving something called 'Spotted Dick', in an establishment with the word 'slug' in its name. It was no wonder that British food had such a lousy reputation.

Anne tucked the menu back between the salt and pepper shakers and ordered a coke. Her companion ordered a pint of Guinness and glugged half of it, wiping the foam off his chin with his jacket sleeve. Anne mentally rolled her eyes. Give him a bandana and he could star in a high-school remake of Easy Rider. A Peter Fonda wannabee. His mother must be so proud.

"So, you wrote that anonymous note," Anne said just to kick things off.

"Nope, not me babe. I delivered it. I didn't write it." He tossed down the rest of his beer and waved his glass at the barman. "We haven't been formally introduced. Name's Billingsley, but you can call me Razor. All my friends do." He stuck out a grimy hand, which Anne ignored.

"Billingsley. Daniel's friend. Didn't the police suspect you of killing Jimmy Soames?"

"Nah, that was all a mistake." Down went the second Guinness. Anne began to wonder who was paying for this little rendezvous.

Billingsley leaned in close to her. "That prick, that doctor, spun them a tale and they were stupid enough to listen. First he tried to pin it on me, and when that didn't work he switched to Daniel."

"But, they have actual evidence against Daniel," broke in Anne. "Some kind of paperweight with blood on it."

"Don't care what they have. Daniel didn't do it. Way too lazy to kill anyone, is our Daniel. Plus, bumping someone off means taking a bit of a risk, and Daniel never puts Daniel at risk."

Anne sipped her coke and mulled this over. The guy was probably right. She couldn't imagine Daniel having the initiative or the guts to kill someone. He could have paid someone to do it, though. She eyed Billingsley warily, glad they were in a public place. "How did you and Daniel meet, if you don't mind my asking?"

"Not at all, darling. My life is an open book." He put his non-Guinness-holding hand on Anne's knee and leaned toward her with a leer.

Anne sighed and jerked her knee away so quickly that Billingsley nearly fell off his barstool. He grabbed the brass rail which ran the length of the bar, righting himself with a good-natured chuckle. Anne got the impression he was so used to being rebuffed that it didn't bother him anymore.

"Daniel and I met on a dark and stormy night in Soho Square. The moon was out, and so were the drunks." He winked at her. "Very romantic."

Anne started in astonishment. "You were lovers?"

Billingsley laughed, choking on the third Guinness he had just ordered. "That's a good one, luv. Nope, sorry to disappoint, but we were just a businessman and his customer. I had a thriving trade in the white stuff —still do – and Daniel was looking to buy."

Anne nodded thoughtfully. That agreed with what Dr. Davidson had told her about Billingsley being Daniel's dealer. Not that she thought either one of them particularly reliable sources of information. "So you didn't know Jimmy Soames, or Daniel, back in your school days?"

Billingsley laughed again, bits of foam flying off his beer glass. "You should be a comedienne, darling. Wyndham Prep. Nope, I'm a Brixton man, me self. Majored in drinking, roach-rolling, and the occasional knife fight." He puffed out his chest – the very picture of a 'West Side Story' gangbanger.

"Did you read that note you delivered to my mailbox?" Anne asked.

Billingsley shrugged and shook his head.

It was the look of uninterested boredom on his face, more than anything else, which convinced Anne he'd had nothing to do with Jimmy's death. "It mentioned Wyndham Preparatory. It also had your address scrawled on the back."

"Yeah, Jimmy put that on, in case you had any questions. You could look me up." He waggled his eyebrows at her.

"So Jimmy wrote that note," said Anne.

"Sure," shrugged Billingsley. "Who else?"

Anne finished off her coke. So. Dr. Davidson knew that Jimmy Soames had written the note. When she'd shown it to him he'd recognized the handwriting. He must have. He'd known Jimmy, what, almost twenty years. She slid her empty glass around in circles on the bar and thought about it. The doctor knew that it was Jimmy who had a grudge against him, who was writing anonymous notes to his neighbors, attempting to ruin his reputation. Trying to link him to something which had happened at Wyndham Preparatory. It had to be blackmail. The doctor had been blackmailing Jimmy for years, threatening to tell the world that Jimmy had strangled a ten-year-old boy. The note showed that Jimmy was beginning to crack. That he wanted out of the arrangement, consequences be damned.

Inspector Beckett and her colleagues in the London police force were focusing on the case against Daniel Soames, but to Anne it looked very much like a stronger case could be made against her next-door neighbor.

Chapter Twelve

TOWER BRIDGE WAS crammed with pedestrians. Anne was swept along by the rush hour crowd as they poured out of the City. She glanced to her right, squinting at the brightness of a spectacular sunset which was just starting to fade. The glass-enclosed sightseeing boats below her reflected back the glare like giant spotlights. At the river's edge the stone walls of the Tower of London were licked by fire as the glowing waters of the Thames lapped at their base. The Tower was peaceful at this time of day, the flags on the White Tower flapping lazily in the breeze. Most of the tourists had left, replaced by pigeons searching for dinner among the cobblestones.

The Tower may have been peaceful, but Tower Bridge was anything but. The giant structure shook as an endless stream of cars and double-decker buses rumbled over it. Anne could feel the vibrations through her feet as she crossed the middle of the bridge. She looked down. Far below her the waters of the Thames rushed, visible through a gap in the walkway. As she neared the end of the bridge Anne maneuvered through the throng until she was at the railing. The staircase which would take her underneath the bridge and over to Butlers Wharf was approaching, but the crowd was single-mindedly following its own path and deviations were not tolerated. At the entrance to the staircase she grabbed hold of its metal banister and swung herself out of the flow like a swimmer fighting the tide.

At the bottom of the steps she darted left and passed through a stone tunnel which emerged into Butlers Wharf. This was a collection of brick warehouses from the Victorian era which had been converted into riverside flats. Their wrought-iron balconies jutted out over the river, the fairy-tale turrets of Tower Bridge looming above. Anne followed the narrow alley at the back of the complex, passing restaurants just opening for business and shops just closing for the day. Most of the businesses were upscale and gourmet, reflecting the income of the area's residents. Cappuccino seemed to be a favored commodity. After a bit of searching she managed to find the entrance to the residential complex. The lobby looked like part of the old loading dock had been filled in and given a coat of paint. Huge beams criss-crossed the ceiling, ropes a thick as a man's arm looped through the gaps. A young woman sat at a desk in the center of the cavernous space. Anne crossed to the desk, her steps echoing on rough wooden planks that were probably the original warehouse floor of a hundred and fifty years ago.

Anne cleared her throat. "Hi. I'd like to visit one of your tenants. Daniel Soames."

"Of course. Just enter his flat number into the intercom." The girl tucked the wad of gum she was chewing into her cheek and pointed to a phone embedded in the desk. "Each flat has an intercom. If he's home he'll answer."

"Um, that's great, but I don't actually know his flat number. Could you look it up for me?"

"I'm sorry Miss. That's not allowed," replied the girl, shifting the gum to her other cheek. "We need to protect the privacy of our tenants. I'm sure you understand."

"Of course," said Anne. "Could you call him for me?"

"Sure, that's not a problem. Your name please?"

"Anne Lambert."

The girl picked up the intercom phone and punched in a three-digit number. Anne politely averted her gaze.

"Mr. Soames? This is Julia from reception. There's an Anne Lambert here to see you. Shall I send her up?" She paused to listen, and then nodded. "I'll do that. Bye."

She rose from her seat and beckoned to Anne. "This way please. I'll need to punch the code into the lift for you. It's part of our security system. Only the tenants can use the lifts."

Anne followed her over to the sleek modern lift which was tucked between two ancient wooden beams and watched her enter a four digit number into a keypad.

"So someone would need to know the code for the lifts if they wanted to get to the underground car park?" Anne asked casually.

If the receptionist was surprised by the question she didn't show it. "Yes. The tenants use these same lifts to get to their cars. Now, just push the button for floor three. Mr. Soames said he'd meet you at the lift."

DANIEL WAS PUFFING away on a Marlborough underneath a no-smoking sign when Anne stepped off the lift. He turned without a word and headed off down the hall, his stockinged feet kicking up tiny blue static sparks on the carpet. He turned into an open door at the far end. As Anne followed him in she gasped. The flat was huge. Small planes could taxi down the living room. The right side of the room consisted entirely of floor-to-ceiling windows. Anne felt herself drawn to them as if by magnetic force. The Thames flowed past at her feet, sightseeing boats crammed with tourists taking pictures of each other circled under Tower Bridge and headed back to Westminster pier. Across the river at angle she could just make out the flags of the White Tower, while directly across the water loomed the modern concrete hulk of the Thistle Hotel.

Anne reluctantly turned from the view to search for Daniel. He was nowhere in sight, but she could hear the clink of glasses in an alcove off the main room. She did a slow pivot in the center of the floor, taking in the décor. There were no carpets, just the original heavy wooden planks, which gave the room an industrial feel. Mahogany leather couches were spread haphazardly around the space, none of them arranged into the conversational groupings so beloved of decorators. Ashtrays littered the end tables, overflowing with cigarette butts. It was unnaturally quiet. Anne guessed that Daniel had convinced Mummy and Daddy to spring for some major soundproofing.

She had just chosen a couch to perch on when Daniel reappeared clutching a whiskey glass. He tossed down the contents and chucked the glass onto the couch next to her. She jumped at the impact but didn't rise from her seat. She was beginning to get a bead on Daniel's personality. He was a common, garden-variety bully, overlaid with a veneer of spoiled rich kid and laced with insecurity. Too lazy to be aggressive, she guessed that he would only become dangerous if backed into a corner. His current demeanor suggested nothing more than irritation at having his evening ritual of smoking, drinking, and most likely coke-snorting interrupted. He had removed his jacket and tie, and one tail of his wrinkled shirt had become untucked from his trousers. He wiped his hands on his stomach, stretching the fabric of the shirt across his thin ribs. He gave Anne a 'get on with it' look.

"I was wondering if you would do something for me," she began. The look on Daniel's face said 'not bloody likely', but she soldiered on. "I'm going to try to get a photograph of Dr. Davidson. A nice clear facial shot. I'd like you to take it to your office. Show it around. Especially to the people who sit near your desk. I want you to ask them if they've ever seen him in your office."

She paused to give Daniel time to take this in. Judging by the lack of animation in his expression, he seemed to be having difficulty. Anne wondered how drunk he was. She was about to repeat herself when he stirred.

"Why?" he asked.

"Why show the picture around your office? Because of that paperweight. The one the police found in Greenwich," she reminded him helpfully. "You said it had come from your desk. So how did it get out in Greenwich? If you didn't kill your brother, then obviously someone took the paperweight off of your desk. Your fingerprints would be all over it. As a tool to frame you it's perfect, but it would have been hard to get hold of without being seen. Most offices in the City have tight security after dark – CCTV cameras, guards, all kinds of stuff. It's more likely that whoever took that paperweight snatched it off your desk during business hours. And someone must have seen them near your desk."

She paused again. Daniel looked more interested in the cigarette he was fishing out of his shirt pocket than in what she was saying. Anne fought a minor skirmish with her temper. This jerk was facing a murder charge. Didn't he care whether he went to jail?

"I'm not supposed to go into the office," Daniel said finally. "Not until this mess is cleared up. Condition of my bail."

"Did they take away your ID, your access card?"

"No. I still have all that shit. I can get into the office, I guess. I'm just not supposed to. Restricted movement the police called it. I'm supposed to stay here at the flat. I can go to Mum's house or to the club. That's about it. Can't leave town, which sucks. Teddy is having a little get together at his place in Oxfordshire this weekend. He always has the best stuff, straight from Columbia. Plus I hear he's flying in some hookers from Hong Kong. Real high-class call girl types."

Anne ignored Daniel's look of intense self-pity. "Will you show the picture around or not?"

"Yeah, sure," Daniel said resignedly. "Doubt that it will do much good though. If you're thinking that the doc killed Jimmy I think you're heading up the wrong road. Davidson protects his own ass. He's a master at it. He wouldn't do the murder thing. It would put his precious self in too much jeopardy."

"Maybe. But it's worth a try. As soon as I get hold of a picture I'll drop it off at the reception desk downstairs." She stood up and handed him a business card. "This is my office number. Call me if you get any results."

"What then?"

"Then we tell the police. Try to point them at Dr. Davidson. I've tried to tell them my suspicions about him, but they seemed determined to focus on you."

Daniel had been walking toward the front door, but now he paused and looked back at her, an oily expression creeping into his drunken eyes. "You seem damn certain that I didn't kill my brother. Has it ever occurred to you that you're making this whole thing too complicated? Maybe no one stole that paperweight off my desk. Maybe I just tucked it into my pocket and walked out with it. Maybe I went to visit Jimmy when he was dead drunk, which was most of the time, and smashed his head in. Maybe I took his worthless little body out to Greenwich and dumped it in the river."

Chapter Thirteen

A NNE PULLED THE fern leaf out of her ear for the third time. It insisted on poking her like a toddler in a bid for attention. She was crouched next to a potted palm and hidden from view – she hoped – by two large maidenhair ferns which were badly in need of pruning. Lindsey was sitting forty feet away at one of the Café Barbican's outdoor tables, checking her makeup with a compact mirror. Dr. Davidson had gone to collect their drinks. The Jose Carreras recital at the Barbican Center was starting in twenty minutes and concert-goers were clustered around the Barbican's central courtyard, smoking, drinking, watching the ducks paddle by in the artificial lake, or admiring the twelfth century façade of St. Giles church. St. Giles was the only pre-1960 structure in the Barbican, and resembled an old woman who had refused to move out of her home despite having her neighborhood invaded by rambunctious newcomers.

Anne re-checked the zoom lens on her camera. It was at its highest setting. She should get a good head shot. Fortunately the recital was an afternoon matinee, so there was plenty of light. She had practiced with the camera in her flat, taking several not-for-the-scrapbook pictures of her living room wall. The clicking sound of the camera had been barely noticeable. She double checked the flash setting. It was switched off. There was nothing to alert anyone to her presence.

Except the duck. A fat mallard waddled up and planted itself at her feet, quacking loudly. It expected breadcrumbs, and when they were not forthcoming it didn't hesitate to voice a complaint. Anne nudged it with her toe. The duck took issue with this and increased the volume. Several people looked in her direction, including Lindsey. Anne hadn't told Lindsey about this little adventure, and wasn't thrilled at the idea of having to explain to her coworker why she was hiding behind a fern kicking a duck.

She bent down lower and tried to reason with the duck, who was having none of it. It pecked at the soles of her Nikes, hesitantly at first, then with gusto. Apparently rubber was a tasty duck snack. Anne gave it another nudge, which only served to inflame its appetite. Finally she scooped the duck up with both hands and gave it a toss toward the lake. It gave an outraged squawk and flapped its wings in protest before assuming a dignified pose on the algae-strewn surface of the water.

Anne peered cautiously through the ferns. Dr. Davidson had returned, bearing two glasses of Guinness, and Lindsey set her compact mirror down. The doctor looked different, and for a moment Anne couldn't pin down the change. Then she realized that he was smiling. Not a full-fledged grin, but teeth were definitely showing. It looked so unnatural on his usually immobile face that she was amazed Lindsey didn't jump up and run away screaming.

She raised her camera as the doctor sat down. He was turned sideways to her. She snapped a profile shot just for the heck of it. He stretched an arm along the table, one finger tracing the back of Lindsey's hand. Anne could feel her stomach turn at the sight. She wondered if he genuinely liked Lindsey, or if he was just making use of her. Their conversation at Lady Soames' house in Regents Park was burned into her mind. The Lindsey Problem had been torturing her ever since. She didn't think Lindsey was in any direct danger, but that didn't stop her from worrying.

There. The doctor had turned in her direction. She aimed the camera at him and took four shots in quick succession, then sat down cross-legged on the ground and checked her watch. She had about a ten minute wait before the crowd on the patio dispersed and made its way into the theater. She shifted on the cold concrete, trying unsuccessfully to get comfortable. Five minutes into the wait a tiny toy poodle appeared around the side of the potted palm. It gave Anne a disgusted look and lifted its leg, wetting the pot with a miniscule stream of liquid before trotting off again.

IT HAD BEEN two days since she'd dropped off the pictures of Dr. Davidson at Butler's Wharf. Two days without hearing anything from Daniel. Anne was beginning to wonder if he'd forgotten all about their arrangement. Finally, on Friday morning she received a call at work.

"It's me."

Anne frowned at the phone. "Who is this?"

"Soames," said the voice impatiently.

"Oh. Daniel. I didn't recognize your voice. How did it go?"

"Barber recognized him."

"Barber?"

"Yeah. Barber. The guy who sits next to me. Not the brightest bulb on the tree, but he says he saw Davidson sit down at my desk, you know, like he was waiting for me. He stayed for a minute or so then left."

"What day was this?"

"What?"

Anne sighed. "What day did Barber see Dr. Davidson? The date."

"Oh. Didn't ask him."

Anne dropped her head into her right hand and began yanking at her hair. "I'd like to talk to Barber. Do you think you could arrange that?"

"Yeah, I guess. Where?"

"It doesn't matter. Anywhere in the City is fine."

ANNE PERCHED ON a stool in Starbucks, watching the pedestrians pass by along Bishopsgate. The men all wore tailored blue suits and the women all wore black pantsuits. Anne watched in vain for a deviation from this dress code. It robbed everyone of individuality, causing them to blend in with the rain-soaked gray streets and the overcast sky. Across the street black cabs formed a line in front of Deutsche Bank. Every so often a fund manager would rush out of the building and leap into a cab, chatting away to an invisible companion, his omnipresent cell phone headset nearly invisible.

Anne wrapped her hands around her Vanilla Latte. The steam rose up and tickled her nose, while the newspaper wielded by the man on the stool next to her tickled her cheek. She scooted away from him and checked her watch. Nearly noon. Daniel and 'Barber' were late. She'd give them another twenty minutes and then she had to get back to the office. It was a good thing that her employers at the Franklin Group weren't the hands-on type of managers. They generally let her set her own schedule as long as she got her projects done on time. Her immediate supervisor wasn't even in the country this week. He was at the company's headquarters in Los Angeles, enjoying warm breezes and sunny skies, Anne thought bitterly, as she watched yet more rain come down and rush into the gutters. Huge puddles were forming at the street corners where drains were blocked. Pedestrians were having limited success at jumping the wider puddles. Anne winced in sympathy as one woman hesitated at the curb, ready to take the leap, only to be engulfed by a wave of water as a black cab sped merrily by and parted the puddle like the red sea.

"Hey, it's us."

Anne turned. Daniel and an innocuous looking young man wearing the omnipresent blue suit, presumably Barber, were standing behind her. She hopped off her stool at the counter and led the way over to a small wobbly table. She set her latte down but then snatched it up again as the table listed, threatening to slosh half her drink into Daniel's lap. He and Barber were both carrying mochas. Daniel slurped his noisily, apparently unfamiliar with the concept of introductions. Anne sighed.

"Hi, I'm Anne. Thanks for coming." She held out her hand, which Barber shook politely. She realized it was just a surface impression, but he seemed a better sort than Daniel. Less rude, less self-involved. He sat patiently, waiting for her to continue.

"Um," she said, uncertain how to begin. "Are you aware of Daniel's problem?"

"His arrest? Sure. The whole office is talking about it. The police came and searched his desk. I was there at the time and they asked me a couple of questions. Had I worked with him long, did I know his family, that kind of thing. It seemed pretty serious, in fact, I was kind of surprised when they let him out on bail." Barber reddened and avoided looking at Daniel, who seemed unconcerned. He had finished his mocha and was busily lighting up a Marlborough, ignoring the disgusted looks from the next table.

"Great," said Anne. "It helps that you're aware of the situation. I won't go into all the details, but I think that someone else is responsible for the murder of Daniel's brother."

"This guy in the picture that Daniel showed me."

"Exactly. You say you saw him at Daniel's desk. Are you sure it was him?"

"Definitely. It's the hair. Not many people have hair that color. It's so pale it's almost white. Anyway, as I told Daniel, this guy came into the office, sat down at Daniel's desk and waited there for a few minutes, then left. It stuck in my mind, because we don't get that many visitors coming into our area. You have to have an employee

ID card to get past the barrier down in the lobby. If you don't have a card then you have to register at the front desk and they give you a visitor's pass."

Anne's head snapped up at the word 'register' and she looked over at Daniel to see if he had caught the significance of it. As usual, he was clueless. Anne mentally rolled her eyes heavenward.

"This registering of visitors, is it written down somewhere?"

"Sure," said Barber. "In a notebook at the receptionist's desk. They write down the person's name, who they're visiting, the time and the date."

"Barber," Anne began. "Sorry, that was rude. I'm afraid I don't know your first name."

"Timothy."

"Timothy, would you be willing to talk to someone at the Bishopsgate police station? There's an Inspector Beckett there who's working on this case. I need you to tell her what you just told me."

"Sure, if you think it will help."

"Great. It's just around the corner from here, across from Liverpool Street station. Why don't we go over there right now?"

Chapter Fourteen

THE NOTEBOOK WAS missing. Inspector Beckett had called with this unnerving, not to mention frustrating, news an hour ago. Anne sat at her desk, staring blankly at the specifications from NatWest Bank which she was supposed to be turning into code. She, Daniel, and Timothy Barber had all trooped over to the Bishopsgate police station and reported to Inspector Beckett. Timothy had described the visit Dr. Davidson had made to Daniel's desk, and had even remembered the date: February 5th, ten days before Jimmy Soames had been found floating in the Thames. The Inspector had listened politely, if not avidly, and had sent DC Singh over to Daniel's office to retrieve the visitor's notebook. DC Singh returned with the news that the notebook used during the month of February had been lost. The receptionist had replaced it with a new one.

"We still have Mr. Barber's statement," the Inspector had said during her brief phone call to Anne. "It does place the doctor at Daniel's office, giving him access to the paperweight which was used to bludgeon James Soames. However, I have to remind you that Daniel Soames could have taken that paperweight from his own desk at any time. It's also possible that Daniel Soames bribed Mr. Barber to come forward with this story about seeing the doctor at Daniel's desk. We've done considerable digging into Mr. Soames' background, and he has a habit of throwing money around when it suits his needs. I have to say, Miss Lambert, that you appear to be somewhat obsessed with the idea that John Davidson is involved in this matter. Your behavior is bordering on harassment. I suggest you back off and let us handle things. All you're doing is giving the doctor enough ammunition to file a libel charge against you."

Anne ground her teeth as she replayed the phone call in her head. The frustration of not being believed was mounting to the boiling point. Dr. Davidson was a threat, she was sure of it. To herself, and possibly to Lindsey as well. It was guilt which was driving her, she knew. Guilt at getting Lindsey involved in this. She got up from her desk, shoving the chair back so abruptly that it banged against the wall behind her.

"Dude, easy on the furniture." Nick came in, munching on a cherry Danish. Crimson syrup dripped from his chin onto his Van Halen t-shirt. He gave the sticky mess an ineffectual swipe with a paper napkin, turning Eddie Van Halen's face bright red. "You look all stressed out. How come you're in such a bad mood on this beautiful day?"

Anne raised her eyebrows and glanced pointedly at the rain streaking down the windows, but the sarcasm of the moment was lost on Nick. He flopped down in his chair and started typing, oblivious to the red blobs of syrup flying across his keyboard. The office supply cabinet was littered with his victims, the last an expensive ergonomic keyboard which was brought down by the whipped cream atop a full mug of hazelnut mocha. Anne sighed and went in search of Lindsey.

Voices drifted toward her as she approached the reception area. Anne poked her head around the corner. Lindsey was simultaneously talking on the phone and making conciliatory hand gestures at a gentleman standing in front of her. Three other people were seated in chairs against the walls. Next to the door a man and a woman were engrossed in a stack of pie charts, and in the corner a man sat by himself, blocked by a ficus tree. All Anne could see of him was a pair of trousers with creases as sharp as a knife edge. As she watched, the legs uncrossed and approached her. The doctor's white-blond hair glowed faintly blue under the florescent lights.

"Hello Anne."

She stared at him impassively. "What are you doing here?" she asked finally.

"I'm taking Lindsey out to lunch," Dr. Davidson replied calmly. "Why don't you join us? We're walking over to Chez Gerard on Bishopsgate."

Anne glanced over at Lindsey, who waved at her before jumping up to escort a client down the hall. She turned back to the doctor. "All right," she said, crossing her arms defiantly.

The doctor chuckled. He leaned in, the lapel of his jacket nearly touching her head. "I'm really not such a bad guy, you know," he whispered.

Anne glared at him but didn't answer. Out of the corner of her eye she saw Lindsey's lunchtime replacement take her seat at the reception desk. Lindsey returned a second later, already clad in her black trench coat.

"She's too young for you, you know," said Anne.

"Who, Lindsey?" The doctor glanced over at the reception desk, where Lindsey was bending over a computer screen, pointing something out to her replacement. "Nonsense. She's twenty-five. I'm only in my early forties."

"Well, then she's too nice for you." With that cheap but inadequate shot Anne ducked back down the hall to her office and snatched up her parka and purse. She waved goodbye to Nick, who was following up his cherry Danish with a container of cold pad thai. He was talking on the phone, and bits of food were flying across his desk like sawdust in a lumberyard. Anne dodged an incoming noodle and logged off her computer. When she reappeared in the reception area Lindsey and Dr. Davidson were standing arm-in-arm, the doctor murmuring something in her ear. Lindsey laughed and gave him a playful little push on the shoulder.

"John was just saying that you don't seem to like him much," she said to Anne with a mischievous twinkle in her eye. "I told him you just need to get to know him."

"I don't think that will help," replied Anne, eyeing the doctor like a vegetarian told she'd learn to love steak tartare.

Lindsey smiled uncertainly at this. She looked about to reply, but then decided to let it go. She turned and led the way down the stairs and out into the rain. Anne pulled up her hood, following Lindsey and the doctor as they huddled together under his umbrella.

At the corner of London Wall and Bishopsgate they stopped to wait for the light. Over the passing traffic, Anne noticed that a construction site which had blocked the sidewalk for the past three months was now cleared. With the scaffolding gone a tiny stone church could be seen. It was barely twenty feet wide, and not much taller. Its roman-arched entrance was hung with a brand new wooden door painted bright blue. A bell tower no bigger than a toaster perched atop its slate roof. As they crossed the street and passed by the church Anne glanced at the sign posted on its door: St. Ethelberga's, built in 1236. A gigantic shadow loomed over the miniscule building. Anne looked up. The City's newest skyscraper, Sir Norman Foster's project at 30 St. Mary Axe. Tiny St. Ethelberga's looked like an ant about to be crushed underfoot. Anne could sympathize.

When they reached Chez Gerard the doctor held the door open. Lindsey gave him a grateful smile as she passed. Anne ignored him. The room they entered was corporate-cozy, with blond wood paneling and small, wobbly tables set too close together. The clientele was dominated by blue suits, with an occasional black pantsuit scattered here and there. When the maitre d' approached them Dr. Davidson stepped forward and asked to have a look at what tables were available. Only three were empty, all about the same as far as Anne could tell, but the doctor took his time choosing one. Anne curbed an impulse to roll her eyes. When the choice had finally been made she pulled off her parka and sat down quickly, snatching up a menu. She focused on it, trying to ignore the way the doctor was helping Lindsey off with her trench coat. His hands were going places not really necessary, but Lindsey didn't seem to mind. Anne heard a stifled giggle and ducked even lower behind her menu.

"The steaks here are very good," said the doctor to Anne when he finally sat down. "It's a specialty of theirs."

"I know," snapped Anne, feeling like a rebellious child but unable to help herself. "I'm going with the grilled chicken."

"That sounds good. I'll have that too," said Lindsey, smiling at Anne.

Anne gave her a brief smile in return.

"Well, I'm sticking with my usual, the Chateaubriand," said the doctor.

Anne surreptitiously checked prices. The Chateaubriand was the most expensive thing on the menu. Typical. A remark Lindsey had made several weeks ago, about the doctor getting most of his lunches from Pret A Manger, popped into her mind. It had seemed so out of character – getting takeaway lunches. The doctor's persona practically screamed three martini lunch – but she hadn't given it much thought at the time. Now it occurred to her that his eating takeaway lunches at his desk might indicate money problems. If he'd been blackmailing Jimmy Soames then that source of income had died with Jimmy. Anne wondered if the doctor was in the process of making another bid on the Soames money. Possibly from Daniel, but more likely from Lady Soames.

"Do I have something on my face? Ink? A speck of dried shaving cream perhaps?"

"What?" Anne asked with a start.

"You've been staring at me as if I were a particularly fascinating animal at the zoo," said Dr. Davidson. "Or a particularly repellant one," he added with his closed-lipped smile.

"I . . .sorry. I didn't realize I was staring." Anne could feel her face turning red, and was grateful that the waiter chose that moment to take their order. She pulled her chair in closer, making room for a couple who were trying to get past to their table. All the tables in the restaurant were now full and the conversational hum amped up another notch.

"I'm glad you decided to join us," the doctor began, raising his voice slightly to compensate for the din. "Lady Soames has been asking about you, wondering if you've done what she requested. You've probably noticed that she can be a bit demanding. She's gotten it into her head that I have some influence with you."

"She'd be wrong," Anne said flatly, looking up from the spot on the tablecloth she'd been studying.

The doctor smiled faintly. "I tried to tell her as much, but she's having none of it. She is insisting that I convince you to go to the police. She's worried about Daniel. The evidence against him is beginning to pile up."

Lindsey frowned and glanced from Anne to the doctor. "Go to the police? What are you talking about?"

Anne hesitated while the waiter set their drinks down. The doctor took up his glass of Bordeaux, watching her over the rim as he sipped. Anne could practically smell the manipulation. He was forcing her hand, setting it up so that she had no choice but to bring Lindsey deeper into this mess. Anne made what she knew was a useless attempt at deflection.

"Lindsey, I've been meaning to ask you how that bid on the Halifax work is going. Do you think we'll get the contract?"

"Don't you change the subject Miss," said Lindsey, waving a finger at Anne in mock anger. "What is this about going to the police?"

Anne sighed and rubbed her right eye, which was starting to twitch. "Do you remember Daniel Soames? The guy who came to see me at the office, the one you didn't like?"

"Sure," said Lindsey. "The cokehead."

Dr. Davidson chuckled.

"It's kind of complicated, but basically his brother was murdered about a month ago and the police think Daniel killed him. For reasons I can't fathom, his mother – this Lady Soames – thinks I have some knowledge about the murder. She's concocted this story in her head about her son mixing with drug dealers, and thinks I know all about it."

"You?" asked Lindsey in surprise. "Why would you know anything about it?"

"I don't know anything about it. That's my point. A point I've tried to make to Lady Soames, with no success."

"Lady Soames has already spoken to the police, you know," said Dr. Davidson with the air of a man saving the best for last. "To an Inspector Beckett. She's given them your name and insisted that they talk to you. I believe she even threatened to call the head of Scotland Yard if they didn't. And that's not an idle threat. She knows him personally. He's been a guest at their estate in Kent several times."

"She's mixing up her police forces," said Anne. "Inspector Beckett works for the City of London police, not Scotland Yard."

"That hardly matters and you know it," said the doctor dismissively. "Lady Soames has gotten it into her head that you can be useful in getting Daniel out of this mess. I suggest you do what she wants. She's prepared to call everyone, up to and including the Queen, in order to see that you do."

"I wonder," said Anne, doodling invisible lines on the tablecloth with her fork.

"Wonder what?" asked the doctor.

Anne raised her head up slowly until she was looking him in the eye. "I wonder who put the idea into Lady Soames' head. This idea that I know something about Jimmy's murder. It makes no sense. You know it, and I know it, yet she seems obsessed with it. The idea seems planted. By one of her friends perhaps."

There. Lindsey was taking a sip of her Chardonnay and missed it, but Anne saw it clearly, brief though it was. A flash of anger had cracked the doctor's mask-like face. Anne wondered how much this lunch was going to cost her.

Chapter Fifteen

ANNE NOTICED THE difference at once. The morning after their lunch at Chez Gerard she was walking to work when she saw Lindsey a few yards ahead. Lindsey's normal gait was the energetic, confident glide of a woman who looked good and knew it. Today the black trench coat was as dashing as ever, the shoes as high and spike-heeled, but something was off. Lindsey's usual ramrod posture was collapsed in on itself. Her head drooped, her shoulders were hunched, her feet dragged. Anne felt a tiny pit of fear open in her stomach. She hurried forward.

"Lindsey, wait."

Lindsey turned, but didn't flash her usual 100-watt smile.

"What's the matter?" asked Anne, dreading the answer.

Lindsey didn't reply. She turned away, but Anne caught the sight of tears forming. She reached out a hand and awkwardly patted Lindsey on the shoulder. "Tell me."

"Last night," Lindsey began, sniffing slightly, "when I got home from work . . ."

"Yes?" said Anne, wishing Lindsey would hurry up and spit it out, as she was imagining all sorts of horrible things and surely the truth was less horrible than the fiction.

"The door to my flat was open. I just froze. I didn't know what to do. I should have gone to a neighbor's and called the police. I know that now, of course. Isn't that always the way? The right thing to do occurs to you way after the fact, when it's too late. Anyway, I just stood there for what seemed like half an hour, then I snuck in as if *I* was the thief – that's what I thought it was – a burglary. I expected to see all my furniture overturned, my grandma's Waterford vase smashed on the floor, my TV missing, but the place looked just like it always looks. Nothing was disturbed. I started to wonder if maybe my landlord had let himself in – maybe there'd been an emergency, a gas leak or something – when I heard the noise. My bedroom closet has a sliding door which rattles when you move it. It's a distinctive sound, not part of the usual creaks and groans of the building. And it doesn't happen on its own. Someone has to slide the door."

"Oh my god Lindsey. Are you saying that someone was still in your flat?"

"I think so. No, I know so. Someone was in the bedroom closet." Lindsey dug into her purse and pulled out a soggy Kleenex. "I ran out of there so fast, you can't imagine. I banged on Mrs. Hudson's door – she lives in the flat below me – but she wasn't home. Mr. McCann lives right above me, but I would have had to go back past my front door and there was just no way, so I ran outside and tried the building next door. I'd never met the lady who answered, but she was very nice. She fed me tea and biscuits and called the police. They came pretty quickly and searched my flat and the rest of the building, but they didn't find anyone. They did take some footprint impressions from the carpet. They said there was a set of footprints made by a man's shoes. John – Dr. Davidson – had been over Wednesday night, but he wears a size eight and these were size sevens."

They reached Britannic House. Lindsey stumbled on the steps, but then seemed to pull herself together. She straightened up and pushed open the heavy glass door to the lobby with some of her usual flair. Anne followed her in. They started up the stairs to the third floor.

"So what happens now?" asked Anne.

"Well, the police dusted my flat for fingerprints. They told me they would call me if they found a match. They also asked me to check with my male friends to see if any of them owned a pair of size seven loafers, but I don't see what good that will do. I know those footprints weren't there when I left for work yesterday morning. My carpet's a pale grey, and footprints really show up on it. They were definitely made by the burglar. Besides, the only man that's been inside my flat recently is John."

"And did the police talk to him?" Anne asked as casually as she could.

"Oh yes. Poor guy. They went over to his flat and made him drag out all his shoes. I'd already told them that the size he wears is too big, but they insisted. I guess they were just being thorough."

When they reached the entrance to the Franklin Group offices Lindsey paused to unlock the door. It was just past 8:00 a.m. and they were the first ones there. The air in the empty reception area was cold. Anne flipped the wall switch for the central heating and Lindsey disappeared into the galley kitchen in the back to start the coffeemaker.

Anne headed down the hall. She absentmindedly turned the light on in her office and sat down at her desk. She stared into space, mulling over Lindsey's break-in. It could have been just a garden-variety burglary she supposed, but an image had flashed into her mind when Lindsey mentioned footprints. The police had found a set of footprints in front of the pier on the Soames' estate in Kent, after someone had tried to drown her. The footprints had matched shoes belonging to Daniel Soames.

DANIEL WAS BACK in jail. It hit the newspapers that afternoon. Anne carried the office copy of the Daily Mail back to her desk.

'Earl's Son Arrested' was the headline. The front page was a rehash of Jimmy's murder. Anne turned to page eight, where the story continued. The reporter indulged in a lengthy description of the wealth of the Soames family, their various holdings in London and Kent, their close ties with the royal family and various Tory MP's. The story then launched into a lurid detailing of the break-in at Lindsey's flat, implying that Daniel was stalking 'a beautiful blonde receptionist barely out of her teens'.

Anne refolded the paper. So, Daniel was again the fall guy, and Dr. Davidson was walking around free as a bird. She felt a sudden reluctance to return to her flat. What if she ran into the doctor in the hallway, or worse, in the lift?

"Hey dudette."

Anne jumped as Nick bopped into the room, the volume on his iPod turned up so high that she could hear it pulsing. Nick gave her a little wave, then paused uncertainly and pulled off his headphones.

"Dude, you look worried. What gives?"

The concern on his face looked strange. Nick was never alarmed, never worried. Anne had never seen him get upset, not even the time he'd spilled a full cup of hot coffee on his lap ('Dude, that was like a real eye-opener. I'm more awake now than if I'd drunk the stuff').

"I'm okay. Really," she added when Nick continued to look at her worriedly. "Hey, it's quitting time. Why don't we get out of here?"

Nick nodded and switched off his computer, grabbing his back-pack off the floor. As they passed the reception desk Anne paused. Lindsey appeared to have left for the day. She wondered where Lindsey had gone. Hopefully she was staying with a friend or relative for a while. Anne hated to think of her going back to her flat, with memories of the break-in all too recent.

Nick led the way out of the lobby and they passed out into the cold evening air. As she paused to let a group of people pass by Anne noticed a dark blue Jaguar parked at the entrance to the building, its headlights illuminating the raindrops which were starting to fall. She heard the quiet whir of an automatic window being lowered.

"You're going to get soaked if you try to walk home. Would you and your friend like a ride?" Dr. Davidson's pale hair shone in the dark interior of the car like snow under a streetlight.

Nick paused uncertainly, but Anne quickened her pace, not looking at the Jaguar. Nick hurried to catch up.

"Who is that guy?" he asked, his head still turned back towards the parked car.

"My neighbor."

Nick looked at her doubtfully, waiting for more details. When they weren't forthcoming he shrugged and walked quietly along by her side. At the entrance to Moorgate tube station Anne stopped.

"Why don't you duck in here and catch your train, before the rain gets worse? I'll be fine by myself the rest of the way."

Nick stared down at her, fat drops of rain carving furrows through his spiky hair. A rivulet of hair gel ran down under the neck of his t-shirt.

"No way dude. Something's going on. I can tell. I've got that ESP thing. I'll walk you home. It's no big deal."

Anne wanted to argue, but she had to admit to herself that she was glad of his company. As they left the shelter of the station's awning she glanced behind her for the Jaguar. It didn't appear, but an uneasy certainty that Dr. Davidson would be waiting for her when she went home took hold. As they got closer to her flat Anne's steps slowed. They were passing a corner pub. Spots of amber light fell on the sidewalk from its leaded windows, laughter floated out the door. Maybe it wasn't safety, but it was a temporary reprieve. Anne grabbed Nick's sleeve and tugged him inside.

THE RED LEATHER seat of the booth creaked as Anne settled in. She took a sip of her Diet Coke, then leaned her head back and closed her eyes. Nick had polished off a pint of Newcastle Brown and was now in search of any food on offer. A tempting smell of fried cod and chips wafted toward their table. The warmth of the pub, combined with the rain pounding against the leaded windows, was hypnotic and irresistible. Anne nodded off.

The scrape of a chair against the tiled floor jerked her awake. She yawned and turned to smile at Nick, ready for her share of fish and chips.

"I'm thrilled that you're so pleased to see me. Quite an unexpected pleasure." The doctor tossed his cashmere overcoat onto the spot where Nick had been sitting.

Anne froze as if her veins had been injected with ice. Her eyes scanned the room, but Nick was nowhere in sight.

"He's in the loo. Maybe it's none of my business, but I have to say he seems a tad young for you. What is he, eighteen, nineteen?"

Anne ignored this, considering escape routes. His chair was blocking her side of the booth. She could scoot all the way around the table and exit from the other end, but it would be awkward and embarrassing. She decided to stay put. It was a public place, lots of people around, and Nick would be back any second.

"You need to leave Lindsey alone," she blurted out. The act of speaking seemed to unfreeze her limbs. She squared her shoulders and twisted in the booth so that she was facing him.

"Do I," replied the doctor softly. "And why is that?"

"I know you've been in her flat. I'll tell the police."

"Of course I've been in her flat. She's invited me over several times. We're dating. The last time I checked it was still legal in England. Though I wouldn't be surprised if the Americans had outlawed it."

Anne took a deep breath before replying. "You hid there yesterday. In the closet. It frightened Lindsey to death." Her jaw tightened in anger. "She called the police and they found footprints on her carpet. Men's loafers. Size seven."

"Dear me. How upsetting. I seem to recall reading something about it in the Daily Mail. Yes, it's coming back to me now. Earl's son arrested for stalking pretty blonde receptionist. Poor Daniel."

He chuckled and adjusted his shirt cuffs by a fraction of an inch. "I have to admit I was surprised when I read the article. I wasn't aware he even knew Lindsey. In fact, I was under the impression that it was *you* that Daniel was interested in."

"Don't be ridiculous. We barely know each other."

"Really. Daniel doesn't normally get many female visitors to his flat – well, except for the kind he pays for – so imagine my surprise when I found out that you'd been to see him."

Anne dropped her Coke can to the table with a clunk. "How could you possibly know whether I've been to Daniel's flat?"

The doctor delicately rubbed his thumb and index finger together. "Bribery, of course. Extremely useful custom. I highly recommend it. Can be adapted to any situation. I make weekly payments to a security guard in Daniel's building. They have CCTV cameras in the hallways. The guard tapes all of Daniel's visitors and sends me a copy. I have quite a collection of hookers, drug dealers, trust-fund trash, and one American computer programmer with lovely green eyes."

"Who has lovely green eyes? Anne does?" Nick set down a pint of bitters and a greasy paper plate overflowing with curly fries smothered in catsup. He leaned over the table towards Anne, peering at her as if he'd never seen her before.

Anne gave him a small, indulgent smile. One of her favorite things about Nick was that he'd never tried to hit on her. She suspected that he considered her too old, which didn't bother her. She also didn't have any piercings or tattoos, which seemed to be a membership requirement for Nick's pool of potential dates. He liked them punky and spunky, with spiked hair, too much kohl eyeliner, and enough metal accessories to make playing with magnets a hazardous under-taking.

"You're right. She does. Huh." Nick sat down with a grunt of surprise, as if he'd just noticed that Anne had grown a second nose. He grabbed a handful of fries and pushed the plate into the center of the table. "Help yourselves."

Anne selected a fry which had escaped the catsup deluge and chewed on it while she considered the situation. She wasn't really sure what to do. Her normal response to Dr. Davidson was always to remove herself from his vicinity as soon as possible, but in this case it was probably safer to stay where she was. She had a nasty feeling that the doctor was planning something. First waiting for her outside her office, and now this little chat in the pub. It would be better not to go back to her flat. She selected another fry and waited.

Dr. Davidson took one glance at the greasy plate of fries and frowned in distaste. His reaction to Nick was about the same. Anne watched them size each other up. The doctor's disapproving reaction didn't surprise her, but Nick's did. He was looking at the other man with dislike plainly visible on his expressive face. This from Nick, the guy who liked everyone he met. Everyone. Even the ancient mail carrier who swore at Lindsey every morning when he delivered the day's post.

"So, you're Anne's neighbor," said Nick, sounding almost threatening. Unfortunately, his tough-guy attitude took a hit when a glob of catsup dripped from his chin onto his T-shirt.

Dr. Davidson watched in appalled fascination as Nick scooped the mess off with his fingers and then licked them clean. The doctor's elegantly-tailored shoulders shuddered, and he took out a snowy white handerchief and wiped his own hands as if they had become dirtied by proxy.

"Why were you waiting outside our office?" Nick asked in the same belligerent tone, ignoring the doctor's fastidious disapproval.

"I was on my way home, and I just stopped by to see if Anne wanted a ride," said Dr. Davidson in a tone which suggested he was struggling mightily to preserve his good humor in the face of an extremely whiny two-year old.

Anne could tell by the blank look on Nick's face that he had failed to find a comeback to this eminently reasonable statement. She could see the doubt creeping into his eyes. Maybe I was wrong, he was thinking. Maybe this guy isn't so bad after all. Anne felt a twinge of panic. She had been so gratified to see that someone else disliked the doctor. Apart from Jason, the art student she'd met at that Tate exhibit, everyone else seemed to find nothing unlikable about the doctor. Nick was an ally, and she wanted him to stay that way. She cast around for something which would turn back the tide.

"I thought you might have been waiting for Lindsey," she said to the doctor before turning a guileless face to Nick. "He's dating Lindsey, you know."

Nick stared at her in disbelief. "This guy?" he said incredulously, pointing a dripping curly fry at the doctor. "No way dude. He's not good enough for her."

According to Nick no one was ever good enough for Lindsey. He was constantly explaining to Anne what Lindsey's man of the moment was lacking. They were all very nice, he was sure, but they just didn't quite meet The Standard. To his credit, Anne didn't think Nick considered himself this elusive standard. He'd never actually hit on Lindsey. It was more a case of admiration from afar.

Another man might have been stirred to anger by Nick's insult, but not the doctor. He shrugged and gave a tiny, impatient wave of his hand as if brushing away a fly. "I need to talk to Anne. Make yourself scarce for a while."

Nick glared at him and crossed his arms, leaning back against the red leather booth. Anne watched as they stared each other down. She'd never seen Nick act like this before. Usually he was so easy going he seemed like a pushover. She wasn't sure she liked the effect the doctor was having on him. She felt as if she was responsible for corrupting an innocent.

After a tense, seemingly endless moment Anne was shocked to see the doctor, not Nick, give in. "Fine. I'll wait over at the bar." He gathered up his overcoat, which Nick had dumped on the table, and disappeared to the far end of the bar, perching on a stool underneath a crooked sign advertising Bulldog Ale.

"Man, what a nasty dude," said Nick, running a hand through his hair and then rubbing off the resulting hair gel on his jeans. "How did you meet this guy?"

"He lives right next door to me in the Barbican. It was kind of hard *not* to meet him." Anne was still watching the doctor. She noticed that the seat he'd chosen was near the front door of the pub. To get out they'd have to go past him. She sighed. Maybe they could out wait him. She waved at a passing barmaid and ordered another Diet Coke. She didn't mind waiting, it was better than the alternative, but she couldn't keep Nick here forever.

"Why don't you take off," she said. "I'm sure you've got better things to do than babysit me all evening."

Nick started shaking his head before she'd even finished. "Nope. No can do. I'm not leaving until that creepy dude does. Like I said before, you don't have to tell me all the details, but I can tell something's going on. He's watching you right now."

Reluctantly, Anne glanced over at the doctor. Nick was right. Dr. Davidson was staring at her. He raised his glass in a salute. Anne turned away. "Well, you shouldn't have to sit here being bored. Why don't you go play?" She nodded in the direction of a group of stockbroker types who were drunkenly throwing darts. The dartboard had only one lonely green dart sticking out of it. The other missiles were scattered over the floor, with a red one hanging from the nostril of a stuffed Moose head over the bar. The pub's other customers were giving them a wide berth.

"Sweet." Nick jumped up and wiped his catsup-stained hands on his jeans. "I'll whup their sorry little arses. If Mr. Creepy comes over just yell. I'll stick a dart up his nose." Nick caught Anne's rather alarmed look. "Dude, not really. I'm strictly non-violent." And with that he marched off to massacre the dartboard.

ANNE WAS REGRETTING her last Diet Coke. She'd been drinking them for two hours now, and she had to pee. Badly. She turned her head slightly toward the bar, just enough to check the doctor's position. He was still there, staring into the mirror which ran the length of the bar behind bottles of brightly colored optics. At first Anne thought he was admiring himself, but then she realized that he was using the mirror to watch her. She sighed and slumped back into the booth. Her last visit to this pub had been several months ago, a birthday party for one of the programmers at work. She tried to remember the layout. The ladies room was at the end of a narrow hallway crammed with boxes of liquor bottles. The hallway didn't lead anywhere – no back door, damn it.

Anne dithered and delayed for another twenty minutes, bladder ready to burst. To pee or not to pee, that was the question. She was worried about the doctor cornering her. He had made no move towards her table after Nick decamped to the dartboard, which probably meant that he had something else in mind besides just a chat. It had to be her visit to Daniel's flat which had set him off. He might even know that they'd shown his picture around Daniel's office. Whatever the cause, she sensed that he was no longer content to patiently wait out events. Maybe she should ask Nick to walk her home . . . no, bad idea. The last thing she needed was for Nick to get into an actual fistfight – or worse.

Finally, bodily functions won out over fear. When a group of women wearing party hats lurched drunkenly past and headed in the direction of the bathroom Anne slid out of the booth and followed. The ladies room they all shoved into was not much bigger than a closet, with only two stalls. Ignoring the tight squeeze, Anne crowded in, squashed between the sink and a large woman who smelled of equal parts Shalimar and gin. Anne jigged in place until a stall was free, then she hurriedly locked herself in. Aah, relief.

She kept an ear tuned to the conversation outside the cubicle. Two other women were still in the room with her. She finished her business as quickly as she could – she wanted some company when she left the ladies room. She was okay so far. The women were at the sink, drunkenly debating the merits of Ralph versus Joseph Fiennes. One lady declared that she'd like to get Joseph alone, while the other insisted that you should never separate brothers. She flushed the toilet and stepped out – into an empty room. The door to the ladies room was just swinging shut. Anne frantically rinsed her hands under the tap then made a dash for the door.

Her cast took the impact. The edge of the door cracked against the plaster, sending a spasm of pain shooting from her wrist to her elbow. There was no room to dodge. Dr. Davidson picked her up and slammed her against the sink, holding one hand over her mouth as he bent her head back against the dirty mirror.

"Stop struggling or I'll break your neck." To illustrate his point the doctor pushed her head down until Anne could feel the edge of the tile shelf which ran behind the sink. It bit into the back of her neck, crunching against bone. She stopped fighting and held as still as she could, though her shaking knees refused to cooperate. She glanced desperately at the door. Where were all the drunks with full bladders when you needed them?

"Now. You're going to tell me exactly what you and that little worm Daniel have been up to. If you scream I'll get nasty." He took his hand from her mouth and grabbed her by the hair, giving her head a sharp rap against the tile.

Anne scrabbled behind her with her right hand, trying to take the pressure off her neck. Finally she found the edge of the sink and managed to raise herself up slightly. At least her whole weight was no longer resting on a tiny point at the back of her neck. "Went to see Daniel," she gasped.

"Yes?"

"Went to look at his car. The one that was used to run me down. Only caught a glimpse of it at the time of the accident."

The doctor's pale eyes narrowed. "Why would you need to see his car? The police have already ID'd it as the one which ran you down. License plate and all."

"Not the car, the garage. Wanted to see if anyone else could have taken the car."

"Really," said the doctor softly. "And what conclusion did you come to?"

Anne winced as his fingers tightened on her hair. "Not possible. Would need access code to the garage lift. Plus security cameras." As she said this the doctor's mention of his bribes to Daniel's security guard flashed into her mind. Of course. Dr. Davidson could have paid the guard to remove the garage tape on the day of her accident.

The sound of voices outside the door caused them both to freeze. The door handle started to turn. Anne watched as an internal debate flickered across the doctor's eyes, and for a split second she wondered if this was it. She was only thirty-three. Way too young. Her scream died in infancy as the doctor's hand wrapped around her throat. He shoved her against the opening door, eliciting angry yells from the other side.

"Stay away from Daniel," he breathed into her ear, his hand crushing her windpipe. "If I hear even a hint of a rumor that you two have been seen together I'll kill you both."

Anne's vision had narrowed to a tiny speck of light by the time she felt the pressure on her throat ease. She lay on the floor of the bathroom, sprawled on the dirty tile where the doctor had thrown her. There were voices above her, but she couldn't make out what they were saying. She didn't care. The only thing that mattered was getting air into her lungs.

When her vision cleared she found herself nose to toe with a pair of lilac suede stilettos.

"Had yourself a little bit of toilet noogie I see. Good for you honey. Nice looking guy too."

There was no adequate response to this. Anne reached up and grabbed the lip of the sink, pulling herself to her feet. She swayed slightly as she checked out the damage to her neck. There were red marks which would morph into purple bruises later on, but they were barely noticeable right now. Anne felt illogically annoyed by this. After what she'd just been through she deserved obvious injuries which would elicit some much needed sympathy. Instead she had a couple of twenty-somethings in heavy makeup smirking at her. Lilac stilettos gave her a thumbs up sign before disappearing into a cubicle.

Anne cautiously pushed open the ladies room door. Dr. Davidson was nowhere in sight. The drunken dart players were also gone. As she approached her booth she noticed a pair of muddy Reeboks hanging off the end of the red leather seat. The Reeboks were attached to Nick, who was stretched out on the seat, snoring loudly. Anne sighed and gave one of the Reeboks a jiggle. Nick grunted and tried to turn over, nearly falling off the seat onto the floor.

"Nick, come on. Wake up." She gave his foot another shake, then went off to find a pay phone. The cab dispatcher told her one of their drivers would be there in ten minutes. When she got back to the booth Nick was sitting up, a dazed expression on his face.

"Dude, that Stolisshhnaya is way intense. Don't usually down the hard stuff. No stomach for it. But Bill and whats-name, Gary, they said I had to try this pepper flavored stuff. Nasty going down, but man what a buzz." Bee noises commenced. Anne lifted her eyes to the heavens and went to find the barman.

The good-natured bar staff loaded Nick into the cab with only minor detours. The longest delay was caused by the window display in a novelty store next to the pub. Toy chipmunks doing the Hula and a drunken IT geek were a dangerous combination. Nick insisted on proving he could Hula with the best of them, be they chipmunks or no.

When he fell asleep in the cab Anne gave a sigh of relief. A drunken Nick was really more than she felt capable of coping with right now. She managed to pry his address out of him before he nodded off, then sat back wearily as they sped toward Bethnal Green.

ANNE GAVE ONE last look up and down the street. The row of crumbling Georgian tenements was quiet, not a car or pedestrian in sight. The traffic had been light as they journeyed from the City to the East End, and she was positive that no one had followed them. The cab driver helpfully dragged Nick out of the cab and propped him up against his front door. Anne gritted her teeth and fished in the pockets of Nick's jeans for his keys, jerking her hand out with lightning speed when a certain region started to swell. When she unlocked the door and pushed it open Nick slid down it and collapsed in a snoring heap in the entranceway. She tugged him until his feet cleared the doorstep, then closed and double-locked the door.

Chapter Sixteen

THERE WAS A cat on her face. Anne grimaced as a whiff of its nether regions reached her nose. Grumpily, she picked up the Persian and dumped it on the floor. It stalked off, tail in the air, apparently used to better treatment.

Anne ran a finger gingerly along the spot on her throat where Dr. Davidson's hand had been. Pain emanated from just below her chin. She was willing to bet that a lovely multi-colored bruise was blossoming there. She sagged back into the broken-down sofa, ignoring the spring which was poking into her left buttock. Maybe she'd just stay here. Permanently. Nick could bring her takeaway curries each night after work. She'd never have to face the outside world again. The cat could keep her company. After it had gotten over its snit.

She was just dozing off again when the sound of retching hacked its way into her consciousness. Nick was awake. Reluctantly Anne sat up, pulling off the Batman and Robin duvet which she'd found in the hall closet underneath the latest issues of British Surfer magazine. Apparently Cornwall was set to knock Maui off the Hot Spots list. Having seen what passed for waves at Newquay, Anne was inclined to doubt this.

"Duuude, what a night." Nick clumped down the stairs and gave her a half-hearted peace sign before disappearing into the kitchen. He didn't show any surprise at finding her on his couch, so Anne surmised that at least a few of his memories from last night remained intact. She pulled up the collar of her parka – which she'd slept in – to cover the bruises on her neck and looked around for a clock. A plastic monstrosity shaped like a can of Schlitz which would have looked at home in any dive bar in Milwaukee informed her that it was ten minutes after nine. Anne had a momentary twinge of guilt at being late for work, until she remembered that it was Saturday. She entertained and then quickly nixed the idea of using the bathroom. A Nick-maintained bathroom was a horror too monstrous to contemplate. She stiffly pushed herself off the couch and wandered into the kitchen.

"Have a seat." Nick helpfully pushed yesterday's Daily Mail and what looked like the remains of a ham and mustard sandwich off a vinyl-covered barstool. Anne hoped the crusty brown stuff in the middle of the seat came from curry rather than cat. It looked dry, at least. She sat down gingerly.

"Das Rheingold?" She asked in astonishment as a booming Alberich started chasing the Rhinemaidens around a stereo in the corner.

"Sure. Old Richard W is great first thing in the morning. I tell you, that Wagner has some bitchen leitmotifs." Nick hopped off his stool and rummaged in a half-height fridge under a sink piled high with dirty pots. "I've got eggs, or I can do you a bacon sarnie." He looked questioningly at Anne.

"No thanks. I'm not really hungry," Anne lied as her stomach growled. She smiled at Nick to show that she appreciated his offer, but there was just no way she was going to eat here. She was no great shakes as a housekeeper herself, but this place looked like Salmonella Central. She glanced around the room. "Do you have a phone I could use? I appreciate your hospitality, and all your help last night, but I feel like I'm intruding. I'll call a cab."

ANNE SELECTED A piece of bread from the basket and nibbled on it. It was a bit dry. She washed it down with a sip of Cherry Coke. The professor had recommended the pub because of its patio overlooking the river. A weak sun shone on the picnic tables, lighting the flower-box full of red geraniums which was hanging over the entrance to the pub. Anne looked enviously at a cozy table by the fire which she could see through the diamond-paned window. Despite the chill in the air the professor had insisted on eating outside so that he could smoke. Anne tucked her hands into the pockets of her parka and shivered as a cold breeze tickled her neck.

"So, how long have you known John Davidson?" she asked.

"Hmm, let me think," said Professor Kenneth Moore, lecturer in English History at Wyndham Preparatory School for Boys. "About twenty years I'd say. Though of course I haven't seen much of him since he left the school, which was about fifteen years ago." He picked up a napkin and dabbed at a splodge of mustard which had spattered his tweed suit.

Anne picked unenthusiastically at her chicken pot pie. Nerves were killing her appetite. She couldn't shake the feeling that back in London Dr. Davidson was plotting something. After leaving Nick's place she'd impulsively hopped a train down to Kent, partly just to put some distance between herself and the doctor, but also with the vague hope of digging up some dirt she could use against him. Professor Moore was her first stop. He'd been friendly when she'd visited Wyndham Prep in the company of Lady Soames, and more importantly he seemed willing to gossip about former colleagues.

"Twenty years. That's a long time. Were you friends when you were both working at the school?"

"Friends? Hardly. Davidson has always been an aloof sort of fel-low. He wasn't close to any of the faculty. The only person he ever spent much time with was Jimmy Soames. In fact, there was some talk about that. Davidson seemed to target the boy. Many of the teachers felt he spent too much time with Jimmy. Oh, the boy had problems, but no fifteen year old boy needs two hours of counseling each day."

"What do you think they talked about?"

Kenneth drained his Guinness and waved the empty glass in the direction of a passing waitress who took it away to the bar for a refill.

"I don't know," he finally replied, gazing down at the reeds lining the river bank. "I'm sure they went into Jimmy's drinking problem. Even at that age he spent most days in a state of heavy picklement."

Anne nodded encouragingly. "Didn't Jimmy have friends his own age he could talk to?"

"Hmm," Kenneth frowned, "Let me think. This was fifteen years ago, you know. Fortunately, remembering names comes easily to a history teacher like myself." He burped in a self-satisfied way. "There was one chap. What was his name. Foxes and chocolate."

"What?" asked Anne, startled.

Kenneth waved away her surprise. "Mnemonics. Attaching vivid pictures to someone's name to aid the memory. Now let me see. Foxes, hounds, fox hunt. That was it. Hunt. And the chocolate referred to a brand name. Godiva, no. Hershey. Thorntons. That's it. The boy's surname was Hunt-Thornton. He and Jimmy Soames were roommates. Not a fact I would normally remember, but it sticks in my mind due to that nasty business I mentioned when you were down here last. You know, the murder of that little boy. Both Jimmy and this Hunt-Thornton were questioned at length by the police."

Anne mentally added the name Hunt-Thornton to her list of people to talk to. The waitress came by and she ordered dessert just to prolong the meal. She decided on chocolate gateau. Kenneth waved away the dessert menu, but held up his pint glass again. Her next question was a bit trickier. She waited until Kenneth was deep into his third pint.

"Was Dr. Davidson kept very busy by the school? I mean, did a lot of the students go to him for counseling?"

"Well, they didn't go willingly if that's what you mean. The only time boys went to see Davidson was when they were in trouble. A teacher, or sometimes their House Master, would order them to go as a form of punishment. Most of the time it was the usual teenage stuff – drugs, drinking, graffiti, fighting. Don't know whether any of the boys were actually helped by Davidson. Just the opposite, I'd imagine."

"Why? Wasn't he good at his job?"

"Well," Kenneth glanced around as if spies were hiding behind the geraniums, "this is just between you and me, you understand."

Anne nodded solemnly.

"From what I heard Davidson was terrible. Absolutely awful at his job. He may be a good psychiatrist, I'm in no position to judge his competency in that area, but I can tell you that he had no talent at all for relating to the boys. There are two ways of going about that." He paused to swallow the last of his pint. "One is the method I and most of the younger teachers employ, which is to befriend the boys, relate to them on their level. The other is the Gordonstoun approach, where the teacher is the classic authoritarian figure whose role is to beat the boys into submission. Davidson didn't take to either of these roles. His main method of approach seemed to be to avoid the boys whenever possible."

"Kind of hard to be a school counselor if you avoid those you're supposed to counsel."

"Exactly. Which is why Davidson didn't last long at Wyndham."

"I thought he was employed there for five years."

"He was. That isn't long by Wyndham's standards. Most of the staff stay there for decades. It's a nice, peaceful setting, and the pay is good."

They were getting off track here. Kenneth looked ready to launch into an endless discussion of the school and its fascinating (to him) internal politics. Anne trawled her brain for a way to steer the conversation back to more productive waters.

"So, were there any kids who got sent to Dr. Davidson a lot?"

"Davidson again. Why are you so interested in the man, if I may ask?"

Oops. Anne started to change the subject, when Kenneth interrupted.

"Hughie Kildare."

"Pardon?" asked Anne.

"Hughie Kildare. He spent the most time in Davidson's office. After Jimmy of course. Hughie was quite the troublemaker. A bit of a con artist. He straightened out though. Works at Wyndham now. In the Admissions office."

Chapter Seventeen

ANNE'S ROOM IN The White Horse Inn had a musty sort of charm. Its four-poster bed had cabbage roses running amok over its canopy and bedspread. The room's mullioned windows were set into yellowed plaster which dropped flakes onto the rough wooden floorboards. The inn was centuries old, with dark beams leaning into one another at unnatural angles and a fireplace down in the lobby which was tall enough to stand in.

Anne dumped her parka on the bed and sat down at a wobbly desk which sported an inkstained blotter and an ancient rotary phone. She opened drawers until she unearthed a tattered phone directory for the county of Kent. Three Hunt-Thorntons were listed, one of them in Fairhill, the closest town to Wyndham Prep. She'd try that one first. She noted down the number and flipped over to the K's. Kent had a whole page of Kildares. No Hugh or Hughie. Not that it really mattered. She could track down Hughie easily enough just by going over to the school's Admissions office. She checked her watch. 4:00 p.m. Mr. Hunt-Thornton was probably at work, but she'd try calling anyway.

Anne picked up the phone to dial, then hesitated. What on earth was she going to say? No plausible reason for asking questions about someone's old school roommate came to mind. After sitting there stuck in indecision for a full ten minutes, she finally decided to go with the truth. She dialed.

"Yes?"

Anne jumped. She'd been expecting an answering machine. "May I speak with Mr. Hunt-Thornton please?"

"Speaking."

"Oh. Hi." Anne could feel her cheeks flush with embarrassment. She stood up and began to pace the room. "Um, my name is Anne Lambert. You don't know me, and this is going to sound odd, but I'd like to ask you about someone who I believe was an old school friend of yours. Jimmy Soames."

The silence stretched out so long that Anne wondered if she'd lost the connection. "Hello?" she asked.

"Sorry. You just took me by surprise. I haven't heard the name Jimmy Soames for quite some time. Well, strictly speaking that's not true. I did read about his death in the local paper. It was on the front page. Any news about the Soames family merits a headline around here. How do you know Jimmy?"

"I met him in London. He was visiting my neighbor, Dr. John Davidson."

A quick intake of breath hissed across the phone line. "I see."

That was all. Just those two words, but something caused Anne to prick up her ears. "Do you know the doctor?" she asked.

"Yes, I do. Well, I did. He was the school counselor at Wyndham Prep. Look, I don't mean to be rude, but what is this all about?"

Anne took a deep breath and got to the point. "When you were at school together, did Jimmy confess something to you?"

"How do you know about that?" His tone not so much offended as wary.

"Well, to be honest, it's sort of a guess. A conclusion I came to from various things people have told me."

"This is all ancient history. And it's not something I want to get into with a complete stranger."

"I know. I understand that. Really. It's just that I'm having some trouble with Dr. Davidson. So, that's why I'm calling. I was hoping you could help."

"I see. No, actually I don't see. What kind of trouble? Is he harassing you?"

"Not exactly." Anne rubbed her left eye, which was starting to twitch. "I believe he may have committed a crime. I think he's dangerous, only I can't seem to convince anyone else of that."

A long silence again. Finally Hunt-Thornton spoke, reluctance in his voice. "Jimmy said he had strangled a ten year old boy. A student at Wyndham Prep. He told me this one day over lunch in the school cafeteria. Just blurted it out. I think he'd wanted to tell someone for a long time, and he just couldn't hold it in any longer. I could tell something was eating at him. He was never a model of restraint, but for weeks before that he'd been drinking heavily, taking sleeping pills but not sleeping, wandering around looking not all there. I don't know if I really believed him about the boy. Jimmy had never been the aggressive, violent type. Anyway, it was too much for me to handle. I was only fifteen at the time. I told him to go talk to Davidson."

"Do you think he told the doctor what he told you?"

"At first I thought that he had. Jimmy started seeing Davidson for two-hour sessions every day. I thought for sure it would come up, but then I changed my mind."

"Why?"

"Because Davidson never went to the police. The investigation into the boy's murder went on for months. The police were at the school every day. Surely if Jimmy had made a confession the doctor would have told the police. Jimmy would have been arrested and the investigation halted. But that never happened. As far as I know the case is still open."

"Didn't it ever occur to you that maybe there was a reason why Dr. Davidson never went to the police?" Anne asked.

"Reason? Such as?"

"Blackmail. Think about it. His patient is an unstable, easily manipulated teenager who has just confessed to murder. The parents of this teenager are extremely wealthy and very high up in the social hierarchy. The boy is terrified of going to jail. The parents want to preserve their place in society."

"Wait a minute. You're making it sound like his parents knew about the murder."

"I think they did, or at least I think Lady Soames did."

"Well, if I were you I wouldn't go around telling people that. The Soames family is very powerful. You could get into a lot of trouble making an accusation like that. Look, I'm sorry, but I have to go. Good luck with . . . well, just good luck."

Anne set the phone down, jarred by the abrupt end to the conversation. She now had confirmation of her theory that Jimmy Soames had confessed to murder, but she had a feeling that Mr. Hunt-Thornton was not going to back her up if she went public with it. And Jimmy confessing to murder was not the same as Jimmy committing murder. He may have fabricated the whole thing in order to appear tough in front of his schoolmate.

She sighed in frustration. She needed something better than this. Otherwise she would be stuck in a permanent state of fear, always looking behind her, afraid to go back to her own flat. She pulled her parka on again, grabbed her purse, and headed out to find Hughie Kildare.

HUGHIE KILDARE WAS ravishing a lollypop. His tongue slithered around the sugary orange undulations, darting in and out like a hummingbird in heat. Finally satisfied, he tucked the candy into his right cheek and answered her question.

"Did I go to see the doc? You bet luv. I was his number one patient. My House Master used to send me to see him at least once a week. Got into scrapes when I was younger. You know how it is." He attempted a man-of-the-world wink, which fell flat. Possibly because he barely came up to Anne's chin and weighed about as much as the average ten year old. He pulled a toothless plastic comb out of his shirt pocket and scraped his hair back into a greasy pompadour, which promptly split in the middle and began to curl on the ends, making him look like the Grinch on a bad hair day.

Anne regarded him thoughtfully. Now that she had found Hughie she wasn't really sure what to do with him. She decided on exploratory surgery rather than the direct approach. "What did you think of him?"

"Of the doc? We got along okay. A lot of people here didn't like him, but him and me were like two peas in a pod, if you know what I mean."

Anne raised an eyebrow.

"We were both crooks." Hughie chuckled delightedly at her surprised expression. "Oh, I don't mean in the legal sense. No, we were both too smart for that. I just mean that we shared a certain outlook on life. We both liked money, and were willing to bend the rules to get it. My specialty was lifting things. You know, stealing. It's amazing what kinds of things kids will leave lying around in their dorm rooms. Cash, drugs, Daddy's credit cards. I had a way with locks too. An uncle of mine, he was a locksmith and he taught me a few things. Wasn't a lock on campus that I couldn't pick. I was always breaking into the school offices. Having a peek in the personnel files, the student records, you name it."

A thought occurred to Anne. "Did you ever break into Dr. Davidson's office?"

Hughie flashed a nasty, knowing grin at her. "Want to see his files do you?"

"Yes," said Anne bluntly. "Of course, they might have been destroyed. The ones I'm interested in are from fifteen years ago."

"Nah, they never destroy that stuff. Keep it forever." Hughie tucked the comb back in his pocket and leaned toward her. "I can get you whatever you want. Files, computer records, session tapes."

"Session tapes?" asked Anne. It sounded like something the school band would make.

"You know. Session tapes. Recordings of the doc's sessions with his patients. He never taped me, cause I knew about the tape machine in his desk. Found it one day while snooping. But he used to tape the other kids. Not all of them. Just his favorites." He paused and looked at Anne slyly. "I bet some of those tapes are worth a good bit. To the right people."

Anne sighed. She didn't know if Dr. Davidson was inclined toward stealing, but he and Hughie certainly seemed to have blackmail in common. "How much?" she asked.

"For you they're going cheap. Just a hundred quid. And a date Friday night. It's darts night at The Bull and all my buddies are going to be there. Last week Ian had a blond on his arm, but she was trashy compared to you." Hughie gave her his best Sean Connery smirk.

"A hundred and ten pounds and we'll skip the darts."

Hughie looked disappointed but not terribly surprised. "It's a deal. Meet me back here at 7:00pm. All the teachers and office staff are gone by then. There's a few guards and cleaning ladies to watch out for, but I can work around that."

IT WAS COLD in the supply room. Anne shivered as she watched Hughie work. They were deep in the basement of the school's Administration building, along with a watchful troop of rodents. Every few minutes Anne would catch one out of the corner of her eye, dodging from box to box like tiny commandos surrounding a village. She assured herself that they were just mice, not rats. Whether she believed herself was doubtful.

"Ouch. Shit." Hughie sucked on a bloodied index finger. "Damn padlock."

"Are you okay?" asked Anne, not really caring all that much, but determined to keep Hughie cooperative.

"Yeah. Sure. Don't worry about it luv. Just nicked my finger." He smirked and held out the injured body part. "Want to kiss it and make it better?"

Anne folded her arms and didn't reply. Hughie grinned at her and got back to work. Five minutes later they were inside. It was the records room. Decades and decades of school records of every description. Piles and piles of boxes. The cautious optimism which Anne had felt ever since her lunch in the pub with Kenneth deserted her. How would they ever find anything in this mountain of paper?

Hughie was watching her with a knowing grin on his face. "Looks like a dump doesn't it? The place where old records go to die. No organization, no system, no index. Nothing except," he paused dramatically, "old Hughie here. You're damn lucky you came to me luv. I know where all the bodies are buried. Over in that corner," he pointed to a sagging stack of faded blue accordion files, "we have every detention slip ever written. The teachers tally them up every semester when they fill out each kid's progress report. I used to make a nice little killing back in my student days. Kids would pay me to steal the slips. Make 'em disappear you know, so little Timmy or Bobby would have a spotless record to show Mum and Dad. Now let's see." Hughie slowly spun around, eyes grazing the cardboard towers surrounding him. "The doc didn't leave much when he quit. He's a careful one. Not much for leaving a trail. But anything he did leave will be over here." He ducked behind a wooden filing cabinet. Anne waited while Hughie shoved boxes around, muttering to himself. Finally he re-emerged carrying a stack of tidy white boxes, all labeled 'Counselor's Office' in block lettering. He pulled the top one off the stack, placed it in front of Anne, and then started nosing around in the others.

Anne knelt down and pulled the lid off her box. Neatly labeled stacks of mint green folders filled it to the brim. Each folder had a boy's name on it. They were in alphabetical order, and she had the A to G box. She replaced its lid and pulled the next box off the stack. H to M. The next box held the S's. Two folders were labeled 'Soames'. One for Jimmy and one for Daniel. Daniel's was slim and contained only three sheets of paper. She scanned them, but nothing of interest popped out. Brief, unconcerned accounts of Daniel's adventures with drugs and alcohol. No solutions were offered. Apparently the doctor hadn't thought rehabilitation was an option. Or more likely hadn't cared.

Anne set Daniels's folder aside. Jimmy's was satisfyingly heavy, but as soon as she opened it she knew it had been sanitized. Like the Soames folder she'd looked through in Dr. Davidson's London office, all the papers in this one had been typed. Probably by a secretary or assistant, which meant that the good stuff just wasn't here. Still, there were a lot of session transcripts. Anne flipped through the pages. They covered a four-year period in the mid to late eighties, when Jimmy was a student at the school. She hefted the file in her hands and debated for a minute. "Do you think I could take this with me?" she asked. "I mean, would anyone miss it?"

Hughie was still rooting through the other boxes and didn't even look up. "Nah, no one ever goes through this stuff. These are the inactive files. Old shit. The active files are kept in the offices. Take what you want."

Anne nodded and closed up the box, setting Jimmy's file aside. She stood and brushed the dust off her jeans. "What about. . ."

"Yes! Score." Hughie's head emerged from the box he'd been digging in. "Tapes. A whole shoebox full. Let's see. 1999, 1995, nope. These are too recent. I guess Davidson wasn't the only one who taped his counseling sessions. You said fifteen years ago, right? Hold on." He dived into the storage box again. "Here's another one." He held up a shoebox and popped the lid. "This is more like it. 1991, 1988, all the way back to 1982. This should do it." He handed the box to Anne.

She chose a tape at random. 1987. In addition to the year, the paper label on its front had a list of names, presumably boys who had been sent to see the doctor. Patterson, Wilmington-Bell, Johnston . . . Soames. Anne tucked the tape into her coat pocket and rifled through the rest of the box. She ended up with six tapes in all. Not many for four years of sessions, two hours a day. She handed the shoebox back to Hughie and thought about it. There had to be more tapes. They wouldn't be in the doctor's office in London. Too public and too accessible. He might have them stashed in a safe deposit box in a bank. If that was the case then she was out of luck. Or . . . Or they might be somewhere in his flat. Close at hand, where he could get at them quickly, destroy them if need be.

"Hey," Hughie broke into her thoughts. "Are we going to stay here all night? You got what you came for, right?"

"Yes."

"Great," said Hughie. "Glad I could help. That'll be two hundred quid."

Anne folded her arms and raised an eyebrow.

"Okay, okay," said Hughie. "Hundred and fifty."

Anne just stared at him.

Hughie grinned. "You're a tough one, you are." He stuck out his hand and Anne placed the agreed-upon one hundred and ten pounds in it.

"Ya know," Hughie drawled, giving her a calculating glance, "if it's dirt on the Soames family you're after, well, I might just be in a position to give you some prime gossip. The good stuff. Grade A."

Anne looked at him skeptically. "What kind of gossip?"

"Only the best," Hughie said importantly. "Me and Dec – that's my mate, Declan Flannery – me and him work weekends at The

Hunt Club, this posh country club a few miles down the road. Dec waits tables at this big clubhouse they have, and I have the valet parking gig. Anyway," he hurried on as Anne's foot started to tap, "Dec hears stuff. He's just a waiter. To them posh types he's invisible. So, a week or two ago, he's working the Hastings Room. The inner sanctum. The holy of holies. You only get into the Hastings Room if your family's been around since good old Willie the Conqueror. We're talking the oldest families in England – the Addingtons, the Finch-Bartons, the Soames."

"And . . ." Anne prodded.

"And Dec is working the Hastings Room, when he hears this big crash. He rushes over and sees china and glass smashed all over the floor. He dodges out of the way just in time as Lady Soames charges past him. Turns out her Ladyship had yanked the tablecloth off the table – on purpose, mind you. Lord Soames and his cousin, that'd be Sir Harry Soames, were just sitting there staring at the mess. Dec started picking up the pieces, mopping up the spills, when he heard Sir Harry say something about how he could understand it. That Lady Soames had never liked him much, and how it was going to be hard for her, having to come to him for money."

"Come to him for money?" asked Anne in confusion. "Why would Lady Soames have to ask a cousin for money?"

"Dunno. Dec says he's heard that Lord Soames is monkeying around with the family finances, maybe even changing his will. The family money was going to Jimmy, at the first born, but now that he's six feet under – who knows? It's no secret around here that Daniel Soames and his mum are tighter than two peas in a pod. They stick together against his Lordship, and maybe his Lordship's tired of fighting them. And, of course, there's the problem of the Doc."

"What Doc? Do you mean Dr. Davidson?"

Hughie looked at her with an expectant smirk. Apparently her free sample had run out. Anne sighed and crossed her arms against the chill seeping into her bones from the frigid basement. A mouse squealed in agony from a corner nearby, crushed in a trap by the sound of it.

"How much?" she asked, trying to remember how much cash she had left in her wallet.

"Fifty quid should do it. No sense being greedy," said Hughie virtuously.

Anne dug into her wallet. She managed to cover it, just barely. The last five pounds were in coin, but Hughie didn't seem to mind.

"Right," he resumed. "Well, everyone in these parts knows that Lord Soames just hates the Doc. Calls him Rus . . . Ras . . . what's the name of that Russian chap? The one that did the Svengali thing on the Empress."

"Tzarina," said Anne. "It was the Tzarina Alexandra of Russia. The guy's name was Rasputin."

"That's the one. Lord Soames thinks our Dr. D. is pulling the same con on Lady Soames. Always hanging around her, inviting himself down to the family estate for the weekend, catching rides in the Rolls. A nice gig if you can get it," sighed Hughie enviously. "There's even some talk that she gives him money. That between her Ladyship, the good Doc, and that little sniveler Daniel, they're running through the Soames family fortune like a keg of Guinness on a hen night. Looks like his Lordship has finally wised up and is trying to protect the family assets by doing a deal with his cousin. If he transfers some of the loot to his cousin's name then her Ladyship can't get at it so easily."

"Hmm," said Anne. "How much of this is guesswork, speculation, and rumor?"

"Pretty much all of it," replied Hughie, giving her a cheeky grin. "Fifty quid doesn't buy what it used to." He shut the file room door and headed for the stairs. "Let's get back above ground before me privates turn to ice and drop off."

Chapter Eighteen

ANNE GOT UP from the desk and stretched her arms over her head. It was late afternoon. She'd spent the day in her room at the White Horse Inn reading through Jimmy's file. Most of it was Jimmy whining about his mother: Mummy liked Daniel better; Daniel always got the good toys. Blah, blah, blah.

She gave the file an irritated shove across the desk and picked at the cast which covered her left arm from wrist to elbow. It was starting to crumble at the edges. One of Nick's doodles was disintegrating. He'd signed the cast and drawn a surfer riding a curl, but the surfer had faded and now his surfboard looked more like a giant tongue going places it shouldn't.

She opened the box of session tapes Hughie Kildare had found in the basement of Wyndham Prep's Administration building. Pushing the first tape into a portable tape recorder, she nudged up the volume. Dr. Davidson's cold voice trickled across the room.

"Yes, Matthew, your mother *is* a bitch. However, sitting here whining about it to me is not very useful, now is it."

Anne stopped the recorder and pulled out the tape. There were four names on the label, with Soames the second one from the last. She sighed. She'd have to do a lot of fast-forwarding and rewinding to hit Jimmy's sessions.

"HE JUST GETS on my nerves, you know?" Jimmy talking.

"Jonathon?" Dr. Davidson.

"Who else? He's just such a white-assed little weasel. Okay, maybe I shouldn't have hit him so hard, but he wouldn't shut up."

"And why did you want him to shut up Jimmy? Did you proposition the boy?"

YIKES. ANNE STARED wide-eyed down at the tape recorder. Well, now she had an idea why Jimmy might have strangled a ten-year-old boy. Apparently Jimmy had pedophile tendencies. She was amazed that the Kent police had managed to keep this quiet. Maybe the Soames family had 'encouraged' the police to leave Jimmy alone. A few large donations to the local police pension fund might have done the trick.

A sudden noise at her door startled her. She jumped, but it was only the day's newspaper being delivered. Someone had slid it under the door. Anne picked it up and glanced at the front page. It was a local paper called *The Kent Messenger*. The articles were mostly rehashes of international events, but there was also a large color picture of Leeds Castle, which was nearby. The caption read: "Lord and Lady Soames hold gala today for RSPCA."

The RSPCA was a large animal-rights organization. Anne had heard of it because Lindsey was a member and volunteered at one of their shelters in London a few nights a week after work. She scanned the article beneath the photo. The Soames were sponsoring a fair on the grounds of Leeds Castle, complete with food stalls, a petting zoo, and pony rides. The money raised was going to a shelter for abandoned dogs. At the end of the article were the names of people who were attending the gala as guests of the Soames family. Amid the 'Sirs', 'Ladies', and 'Earls', two names jumped out at her: 'Dr. John Davidson, Esquire' and 'Miss Lindsey Maxwell'.

ANNE JUMPED DOWN from the bus and squinted as the dust kicked up by its departure blew in her face. Across the road stretched a field of green vines. The leafy vines appeared to be floating in mid-air, but a closer looked revealed a support structure of strings descending from tall wooden poles. A hop field, she decided. This area of Kent was famous for hops, used in brewing beer. A gravel drive just past the hop field was marked as the entrance to Leeds Castle. In the distance she could make out a familiar-looking stone gateway. It was the entrance to the Soames estate, which bordered the grounds of the castle.

Dodging across the highway, Anne hurried past a flustered attendant who was trying to organize the stream of cars funneling into the parking area. She'd been to Leeds Castle once before. After moving to London she'd spent her weekends taking the train to various castles, cathedrals, and other tourist sites. Leeds Castle had been one of the most enjoyable outings. It had extensive grounds, with the obligatory maze, an aviary, a croquet lawn, and a thousand-year-old Keep situated on an island in the middle of the River Len. The castle had been in continuous use for its entire existence, so the keep and its various outbuildings were in good repair. The last private owner had been Lady Baillie, who had redecorated the interior in the 1920's.

Anne left the parking area and cut across the wide parkland surrounding the castle. As she walked through the wet grass she kept a wary eye out for goose droppings. Huge numbers of Canadian geese were waddling randomly around the grounds or gliding on the river. The geese mostly ignored her, though honking commenced if she stepped too near a gosling. It was spring, and little broods of the fuzzy youngsters were following their parents in single-file or hiding under maternal tail feathers.

She stopped at the river's edge, next to a clump of daffodils waving in the morning breeze. The castle was directly across from her, the sun warming its stone turrets. The oldest part, built in 1119, formed an island made of stone. It had small windows and thick walls, sure indicators that it had originally been used as a fortress and place of refuge in times of danger. This older building was connected to a large manor house by a double-arched stone bridge. The manor house was built of gold-colored stone, with large windows and fanciful turrets added as decoration rather than defense. In front of the manor house was a circular lawn where a cluster of colorful tents had been set up, their tops crowned with pennants fluttering in the breeze. A steady stream of people were issuing from the car park and heading toward the tents. Anne joined them.

SHE WOVE THROUGH the crowd, the hood of her parka pulled up to hide her face, trying to catch sight of Dr. Davidson or Lindsey without being spotted. Her plan, such as it was, involved trying to keep an eye on Lindsey while avoiding the doctor. She couldn't shake the feeling that the doctor intended to use Lindsey as some kind of bargaining chip, a shield between himself and the consequences of Jimmy Soames' murder.

After a full pass around all the stalls selling scones, handmade jams, knitwear, and other local crafts there was no sign of them. Anne stopped searching momentarily to grab a Cornish pasty from a food vendor. As she ducked behind the stall to get out of the way of the crowd, yelling suddenly erupted from within the neighboring tent. The loud, angry cries rose above the din of the crowd, causing those in the near vicinity to pause, trying to locate the source of the noise. Anne recognized the voice at once. It was Daniel Soames, broadcasting his usual alcoholic belligerence. The yelling stopped abruptly, and in the ensuing silence Anne could hear someone reasoning with Daniel. She cautiously approached the tent where the sound had come from and put her ear to the canvas wall.

"Manners, Daniel," she heard a voice say softly.

Anne held her breath. It was Dr. Davidson.

Daniel Soames grumbled something she couldn't make out, then doctor spoke again, his voice calm and just above a whisper.

"Except for that marble paperweight, most of what they have is circumstantial. If your case goes to trial now it could go either way. They need more evidence . . . and I'd be only too happy to help."

"What the hell does that mean?" asked Daniel. His voice was still angry, but he'd turned the volume down.

"It means I have things I could share with them. These, for instance."

Anne heard paper rustling and then a sharp intake of breath from Daniel.

"How did you get these?" The belligerence had peeled away, leaving only shivering and exposed fear. "No one has access to my email account at work except me."

"That's not true actually," said the doctor in a helpful tone. "All offices have an email administrator. Someone who sets passwords and creates user accounts. Your company really should look into hiring another administrator. The one you have now is pathetically easy to bribe."

"You've got to understand," pleaded Daniel. "I was just joking around. Teddy knew that. He told me he'd deleted these emails. He knew I was just blowing off steam. Jimmy had been getting on my nerves that week, always coming around to my flat, hanging around drinking my booze, whining about his problems. When I said I felt like offing him I didn't mean it. Everybody says that kind of thing sometimes."

"Maybe," said the doctor complacently, "but most people have the sense not to say it in an email. I'm not suggesting you confess to murder. Just tell the police that you and Jimmy argued and it got out of hand. An accident which occurred in the heat of the moment. You could even throw in an element of self-defense. Your mother will buy you the best criminal defense barrister available, you'll plead to manslaughter, and be out in two years. It's possible you won't serve any jail time at all."

"Jail time! I can't. I won't. You can go to hell. A bunch of emails aren't going to make me turn myself in to the police."

"It's true that they aren't much by themselves. Of course, I could always point the police to the eyewitness. The one who saw you hit Jimmy with that paperweight and push him into the Thames."

"That's a load of crap, and you know it," sputtered Daniel. "There's no eyewitness who saw me kill Jimmy, because I *didn't* kill Jimmy."

Dr. Davidson said something which Anne couldn't catch. She leaned in closer to the wall of the tent, jerking back suddenly when she realized that she was pushing against the canvas, possibly making her outline visible from within the tent.

"Anne! What are you doing here?"

Anne spun around, heart pounding. She was face to face with Lindsey, who was sporting a tailored trench coat, knee-length suede boots, and a very surprised look.

Anne gaped at her, painfully aware that she hadn't prepared an excuse for her presence at the castle. Even worse, she suddenly realized that the conversation inside the tent had ceased.

They came around the corner of the tent before she had time to react. Dr. Davidson was in the lead, with Daniel Soames following him like an out of temper sheepdog. Daniel's hair was sticking straight up and his rumpled suit was covered in what looked like bits of hay from the pony ride. The doctor was his usual dapper self in a spotless cashmere overcoat. He started at the sight of her, but recovered quickly.

"Well, this is a pleasant surprise," he said, sliding an arm around Lindsey's waist. "I didn't realize you were down in this part of the country, Anne. Did Lady Soames invite you to her little gathering?"

Anne was spared from having to reply by the appearance of Lady Soames herself, looking extremely irritated at having to tromp through the wet grass.

"Daniel! What on earth are you doing skulking about like this? The Earl of Wessex has been asking for you. He's up at the banqueting hall, having a civilized cup of tea, not out here playing crude fairground games, or whatever it is you've been up to." Lady Soames paused, peering nearsightedly at Anne. "Miss Lambert, isn't it?"

Anne nodded, watching as the expression on Lady Soames' face changed from irritated to wary. Anne realized that Daniel's mother must have remembered who she was, i.e., the person who'd been run down by her son's car. It looked like Lady Soames was still on guard against imaginary lawsuits.

Lady Soames cleared her throat and fixed on a strained smile. "Miss Lambert, why don't you join us in the banqueting hall? The caterer has done some lovely petit fours."

Much to Anne's surprise Lady Soames linked arms with her and led the way toward the castle. As they merged into the crowd Anne looked back. Dr. Davidson and Lindsey were following arm in arm. Daniel stomped behind them, shooting enraged glances first at her and then at the doctor. They skirted the croquet lawn in front of the manor house and passed through a small person-sized door cut into the heavy oak of the massive medieval doorway.

Lady Soames led the way through a maze of corridors and into the banqueting hall. The huge room had a walk-in stone fireplace and a heavy-beamed ceiling. Its walls were covered with portraits of long dead royalty and a large bow window overlooked the grounds. Round tables with six place-settings each were draped in spotless white tablecloths. Centerpieces of pink roses added to the civilized ambience. As they took their places at an empty table Anne couldn't help wishing that the company was as civilized as the setting.

Daniel sprawled in a chair, picking his nose. Lady Soames patted her carefully coifed hair and muttered half-audible remarks about the rudeness of the Earl of Wessex and his disappearing act. Dr. Davidson threw his cashmere overcoat across an empty chair and stared at Anne with a mocking expression while stroking Lindsey's arm with a pale hand.

"Tea!" shouted Lady Soames suddenly at a passing waiter, causing him to drop the tray loaded with scones and clotted cream he was carrying. It crashed onto the wooden floor, scattering blobs of cream in all directions. Lady Soames shrieked as a splodge hit her in the face, while Daniel casually scooped up a scone off the floor and proceeded to munch on it. Dr. Davidson, whose elegantly tailored suit had escaped the carnage, rushed to Lady Soames' side, dabbing at her face with a handkerchief he whipped out of his breast pocket.

Seeing her chance, Anne leaned toward Lindsey. "Tell them you have to use the restroom."

"What?" asked Lindsey absentmindedly, absorbed in checking her sea-green silk dress for spots of cream.

"You have to use the restroom," hissed Anne more insistently.

"Oh, no thanks. I'm fine," responded Lindsey, pulling a compact mirror out of her purse. "You go ahead if you want to. I think it's down the hall to your left." She scanned her flawlessly made-up face for cream damage. Finding none, she lowered the mirror. "By the way, it's kind of weird, isn't it, both of us spending our weekend down here. I'm beginning to think John was right about you. He says you've taken to following him about." Lindsey's wide blue eyes looked up in concern, as if she was having doubts about Anne's sanity. "Of course, being a psychiatrist he's used to having patients become obsessed with him, but you're not a patient. You should know better. I know I helped you sneak into his office, but that was wrong of me. I realize that now. John has mentioned that he's starting to feel harassed by you."

Anne let out a small groan of frustration. "Lindsey . . ." she said, but was interrupted by the arrival of a waiter bearing a pot of tea.

Dr. Davidson took it upon himself to pour. He served Lady Soames, Lindsey and Anne, leaving Daniel to fend for himself. As he passed Anne a cup of steaming Earl Grey his transparent grey eyes stared into hers. "So," he said, "why *are* you down here in Kent this weekend? It's quite a coincidence, finding you here."

"I saw a notice in the paper," said Anne, thinking quickly while taking a sip of tea. "About a fundraiser for the RSPCA being held here at Leeds Castle. I've always wanted to see the castle, and I've heard good things about the RSPCA from Lindsey, so I just hopped on the train and came down." She paused, sniffing at her tea. It tasted strange. Earl Grey wasn't her favorite, but this tasted even worse than usual.

"Is something wrong?" asked the doctor.

"Yes," said Anne quickly. She noticed that both the doctor and Daniel were staring at her intently, but there wasn't time to wonder what they were up to. This was her chance to get Lindsey away from them. "I'm not feeling well all of a sudden. A bit dizzy. I think I'll just splash some cold water on my face. Lindsey, would you come with me to the Ladies Room?"

Lindsey immediately looked concerned, her previous irritation disappearing without a trace. "Of course," she said, putting a hand on Anne's arm to help her up.

Anne tried to fake a wobble in her step, but found to her surprise that there was no need. A genuine dizziness was engulfing her, as if she'd been drinking heavily. She was vaguely aware of leaning on Lindsey as she stumbled out of the banquet hall. The last thing she remembered was the sign on the door to the Ladies Room. It was floating in the air, its letters stretched like taffy.

"FOUR MINUTES," SAID Daniel, sounding pleased about something.

"Fast-acting stuff."

"What is?" Anne managed to choke out. Her tongue felt thick, her mouth dry.

"The drug. GHB. Hard stuff to get hold of, you know. It's illegal in the U.K. But it was easy for him, being a doctor and all."

Anne felt a hand grasp her hair, lifting her head up. She tried to reach up and swat it away, but her arms wouldn't move. Her body felt like molten lead poured into a misshapen mold.

"It was Mum, you know," Daniel whispered in her ear. "She's the one who bonked Jimmy on the head and pushed him into the river. My Dad was getting wise to her and the doc siphoning off the family funds. Dad started putting things in Jimmy's name. Mum couldn't have that. Neither could I." The whisper turned to whine. "I mean, a chap's got to have cash, doesn't he? Why should that twat Jimmy get it all?" The hand slammed Anne's head on the ground for emphasis. "Course, I wasn't too happy when the doc tried to pin things on me, with that paperweight from my desk. But we've worked things out. The doc's a wanker, but I gotta hand it to him, he's got real talent when it comes to getting money out of people."

Anne felt the hand release her hair.

"Time to go. They're going to open the weir. Irrigation, you know. It always causes a bit of rise in the water level around these parts. The river's already coming in, and these are brand new shoes. Five-hundred quid. Wouldn't do to get them wet."

His footsteps moved away, making a squelching sound. Overhead there was a muffled boom, as if something heavy had been dropped. Even through her closed eyelids Anne could tell that the light had been shut out. She slowly opened her eyes, but it was as dark with her eyes open as with them shut. Slowly she raised herself to a sitting position. Her head was throbbing, and her legs were shaking. The drug must have been in the tea, she thought fuzzily. Dr. Davidson had somehow managed to slip it into her cup when he'd passed it to her.

She tried to stand but her head collided with something – the place she was in had a ceiling only a few feet high. Anne felt along the wall behind her. It was made of rough stone blocks at least a foot square. She was most likely still in the castle. Down near the river, judging by the rank smell of rotting weeds and algae. The ground felt sticky underneath her feet – she was standing in mud.

"Hello?" she shouted as loudly as she could. "Can anyone hear me?" Her voice sounded deadened, as if she was in a sound-proof room. No one answered. "Help!" she screamed. Nothing.

Anne moved along the wall in a crouch, one hand tracing the stones. There had to be some kind of exit. After all, Daniel had gotten out.

Her foot found the answer before her hand. Swearing at the pain in her toes, she felt along the ground. It was a stone step. She cautiously climbed up onto it, stretching one arm above her head. The staircase wasn't long, only five shallow steps. The low ceiling descended upon her as she climbed. At the top of the stairs the ceiling changed to rough, splintery wood. A trapdoor. That was what had made the booming sound when Daniel left. Anne pushed at it, first with her hands and then by bracing herself against the wall and shoving with her shoulders. At first she thought she was making progress. The wood creaked and groaned, raising up half an inch or so. But she couldn't raise it any further. A weight, a latch, something was holding it down.

Anne banged on it with her fist. "Help! Is anyone up there?"

No answer.

She sat down shakily on the stairs and tried to think. How long had she been unconscious? If it was only an hour or so then there would still be lots of people milling around the castle and the grounds. Leeds Castle was not that big. Surely someone would eventually happen by and hear her. She would just have to keep shouting. She opened her mouth to take a deep breath when a sudden rush of water from down below in the dark caused her to gasp in surprise. The cold water washed over her legs, soaking her shoes and jeans before receding again into the darkness. Anne scrambled up as far as she could, her head bumping against the trapdoor.

"Help!" she cried. "Down here!"

She had just twisted around to try and shove at the trapdoor with her feet when the water rushed in again. This time it submerged the entire chamber, washing over Anne and lifting her up until her head bumped painfully against the ceiling. Before she had time to panic the water receded as quickly as it had come, dumping her back onto the steps where she lay gasping for breath. As she pulled herself to a sitting position she realized to her horror that one hand was still underwater. The water hadn't emptied completely this time. The next onslaught might fill the room for longer than she could hold her breath.

She kicked ferociously at the trapdoor, pounding on it in frustration. "Down here! Anyone! Hurry!"

A murmur of voices suddenly floated down into the chamber. Anne froze. Someone was nearby, directly over her head by the sound of it. The heavy wood of the trapdoor muffled the voices, but someone was definitely there.

"Did you hear that?" said one of the voices. The voice was faint and hard to make out, but it sounded like Lindsey.

Anne sobbed with relief. "Lindsey," she shouted hoarsely, "I'm down here. Open the trapdoor. Hurry!"

"No darling," said another voice. "I didn't hear anything." It was the doctor.

"Are you sure?" asked Lindsey's disembodied voice. "I could have sworn I heard someone shouting just now. They sounded distressed. Maybe we should notify someone. A security guard or something."

"No need for that," said Dr. Davidson soothingly. "It's probably just someone partying a bit too hard. One of the booths at the fair is selling shots of Scotch. Glenlivet, I believe. I told Lady Soames that having hard liquor at the event was a mistake, but Daniel managed to convince her otherwise."

"Okay," said Lindsey doubtfully. "I'm sure you're right. We'd better get back. Lady Soames is probably wondering where we've disappeared to."

"No!" shouted Anne, pounding on the trapdoor. "Lindsey, it's me! I'm trapped and water's coming in. You need to get me out of here!"

She paused, her breath coming in panicked gulps. There was no sound from above. She yelled again just as another flood rushed in. She barely had time to take a deep breath and put her arms around her head before the water submerged her. It had increased in volume and violence, flinging her from one side of the small chamber to the other. Anne fought an urgent need to open her mouth and fill her lungs with air. In the chaos of the churning water she couldn't tell up from down. She made a guess at where the ceiling was and tried to surface, but there was no room. Her reaching fingers felt a tiny gap of air between the water and the wood of the trapdoor, but it wasn't wide enough for her to take a breath.

The strain of holding her breath was becoming unbearable. Zigzags of colored lights flashed in front of her eyes. She had only a few more seconds before she wouldn't be able to hold her mouth closed any longer. Water would rush into her lungs, and she would drown. The urge to just get it over with was intense. Anne clamped her teeth shut, biting down so hard on her lower lip that she could feel a warm trickle of blood in her mouth.

She shut her eyes and tried to calm her thrashing arms. She floated, waiting for the inevitable. Drowning was supposed to be relatively painless.

A sudden rush of water took her by surprise. She opened her eyes. The chamber was no longer pitch black. A square of light had opened right above her head. Water flooded up and out of the chamber, carrying her with it.

Hands grabbed her arms, pulling her through the trapdoor and laying her down on wet stone as rivulets of water from the chamber splashed around her.

"Breathe!" she heard someone say.

Anne felt hands pulling frantically at her jaw, and she realized that she still had her mouth clamped shut. She opened it, a shuddering gasp racking her whole body. Blood trickled from her mouth and she felt someone press a cloth to her bottom lip.

"Just lie still. I'll call an ambulance."

Anne squinted up at the person bending over her. Sea-green silk trailed in the puddles on the stone floor.

"Lindsey?" Anne gasped. "But, you left. I heard you. The doctor said something about Scotch and you both left."

"Yes, I left," said Lindsey. "But I came back. Obviously."

Chapter Nineteen

"SO LINDSEY SAVED your life. Cool." Nick gave Lindsey a playful punch on the arm.

Lindsey raised one perfectly arched eyebrow at him. Nick turned beet red and put both hands behind his back.

"Junior," she said, "Gentlemen do not punch ladies. Not even in jest."

Nick nodded vigorously in agreement and clasped his hands together even more tightly behind his back. He stood at attention while Anne and Lindsey settled themselves on a park bench. It was a rare sunny day in London, and Lindsey had suggested a picnic in the park outside their office.

Anne took a bite of her sandwich, watching the sun flash off the silver boules rolling along the bowling green in the middle of the park. Every so often a bowler would make an especially good shot and a sharp metallic click would reverberate through the air as two boules collided.

"So, these two dudes," said Nick cautiously, glancing sideways at Lindsey to see if he had permission to speak.

Lindsey gave him a regal nod.

"So, these two dudes," Nick repeated, "they're going away for life?"

"No," said Anne, "not for life. Since they didn't actually kill anyone they can't be tried for murder."

"But what about that Jimmy dude?" asked Nick, pulling a can of Pepsi out of the pocket of his very baggy surfer shorts. "Didn't they do him in?"

Anne shook her head. "No, his mother did. Lady Soames. She hit him over the head with a paperweight and pushed him in the Thames. It's hard to believe that a woman could kill her own child, but she apparently confessed. I read in the paper that she's trying for a psychiatric defense. Not in her right mind at the time and all that."

"But," said Nick, frowning as he opened his Pepsi, "this Dr. Davidson guy, he needs to be locked up. I met the dude, remember? In the pub. I could tell he was no good just by looking at him. Slimy bugger, I said to myself, soon as I saw him."

Lindsey's cheeks went a delicate shade of pink. "Well, I couldn't tell he was a slimy bugger just by looking at him. After all, I dated him for more than a month."

"It's a guy thing," Nick pronounced. "We can tell right away when another guy's rotten." The expression of deep wisdom on his face was somewhat marred by the fact that he was wearing a t-shirt which said 'Save the Ales'.

"The doctor might not have killed anyone, but he'll still get jail time," said Anne, with more confidence than she felt. Inspector Beckett had called her that morning to tell her that Dr. Davidson was out on bail. The police were concentrating on building a case against Daniel Soames. They had charged him with two counts of attempted murder – the hit and run in London, and the attack at Leeds Castle. Anne wasn't sure about the hit and run. Daniel might have been acting on his own initiative there. But she was certain that Dr. Davidson had been behind the attempt to drown her at the castle. Daniel himself had told her that the doctor had procured the drug they'd knocked her out with. She'd mentioned that in her statement to the police, but she had the uneasy feeling that they didn't believe her. Or if they did, they didn't feel they had enough evidence to pursue a case against the doctor.

"Well, I hope so," said Nick. "They need to throw him in the clink, throw the book at him, hang him by his thumbs." He laughed, snorting Pepsi out his nose. "Hang him by his thumbs. I'd pay good money to see that. And I'd bring along some rotten tomatoes to throw at him too."

Lindsey frowned at him. "There's no need to be callous or crude. Several years in jail will be sufficient for John, I mean for Dr. Davidson. As for the other man, that Daniel Soames, I can't help feeling that he was the true instigator of all the violent acts. Maybe not his brother's murder, but certainly he was the one who tried to run Anne down, and to drown her. I hope he gets a very lengthy sentence."

Nick nodded in agreement, as he always did at any remark of Lindsey's, but Anne noticed that his right hand was still making little throwing motions.

Anne finished her sandwich and leaned back against the bench. Daniel Soames was in jail, and so was his mother. She might have to testify at their trials, but otherwise she could safely forget about them.

As for Dr. Davidson, she wasn't happy that he was out on bail, but on the plus side she hadn't seen any sign of him. She'd overheard Mrs. Watson gossiping about him with the porter in the lobby of her apartment building. Apparently the doctor was four months behind on his rent and the building's owner was starting eviction proceedings. She wondered if he'd left town – or even left the country. She was as eager to see justice done as the next person, but the idea that the doctor had eluded the law and was now halfway across the world was extremely appealing. As long as he was as far away from her as possible she could forgo revenge.

She might spend the next few months looking over her shoulder, wondering if he was somewhere back there, but gradually the feeling would fade. Life would return to normal.

A gentle breeze was blowing, and the spring sunshine was encouraging a few purple and white crocuses to poke out of the dark soil surrounding the bowling green. Anne closed her eyes and breathed a sigh of contentment. Maybe life wasn't quite normal yet, but it was definitely headed in the right direction.

The End

Other books by Kris Langman

The Danger Down Under (book #2 in the Anne Lambert Mystery series)

The Gostynin Shul – a Yiddish History Mystery

The Logic to the Rescue series
Logic to the Rescue
The Prince of Physics
The Bard of Biology
Mystics and Medicine
The Sorcerer of the Stars
Warlock of the Wind
The Engineer of Evil
Math and Manners

Milton Keynes UK
Ingram Content Group UK Ltd.
UKHW050203130724
445574UK00014B/769